The Trouble with Turkeys

by

Kathi Daley

This book is dedicated to my littlest angel Xavier; forever in our minds, forever in our hearts.

I also want to thank Christy for her valuable feedback and help with the recipes, Ricky for the webpage, Cristin for her recipes and encouragement, Paul for his help and guidance, Randy Ladenheim-Gil for the editing, and last but not least my super-husband Ken for allowing me time to write by taking care of everything else.

Books by Kathi Daley

Come for the murder, stay for the romance.

Buy them on Amazon today.

Paradise Lake Series:

Pumpkins in Paradise
Snowmen in Paradise
Bikinis in Paradise
Christmas in Paradise
Puppies in Paradise – *February 2015*

Zoe Donovan Mysteries:

Halloween Hijinks
The Trouble With Turkeys
Christmas Crazy
Cupid's Curse
Big Bunny Bump-off
Beach Blanket Barbie
Maui Madness
Derby Divas
Haunted Hamlet
Turkeys, Tuxes, and Tabbies
Christmas Cozy – *November 2014*
Alaskan Alliance – *December 2014*

Road to Christmas Romance:

Road to Christmas Past

Chapter 1

"This had better be good," I growled as I was rudely awakened from a deep, peaceful slumber. The view from the loft of my boathouse revealed a dark horizon and I was not amused.

"Hey, Zoe. Sorry to call so early," Jeremy Fisher, my ex-assistant apologized.

I groaned as I sat up and looked at the bedside clock. Although the sun had yet to make an appearance over the distant mountain, the digital readout informed me that it was nearly seven o'clock. It happens that way as autumn gives way to winter. Ashton Falls, the village I call home, is nestled snuggly within the protective arms of the surrounding mountains that rise to a height of over ten thousand feet. As the days shorten it takes the welcoming sun a bit longer to rise over the summit.

"I think I found us a job," Jeremy continued. "It's only temporary, ten days; two weeks at the most, but the pay is good."

"How good?"

Jeremy quoted an amount that caused me to gasp as images of the type of job that might pay that kind of money filtered through my head. "You haven't gotten us into something illegal or immoral, have you?"

"No, I can assure you the job is perfectly legal."

"Who would pay that much money for two weeks' work?" I had to ask.

Jeremy hesitated. "A farm in the valley. The owner was found dead in his kitchen yesterday morning, and they need someone to take care of the animals until . . . until other arrangements can be made."

"Where in the valley?" I yawned.

"About twenty miles south of Bryton Lake."

Bryton Lake is thirty miles away, which would put the farm a good fifty miles from my mountain home. The fact that I'd be required to spend two hours commuting between the two locations every day didn't thrill me, and I suspected Jeremy knew that.

"Please think about it at least," Jeremy pleaded.

"Yeah, okay." I yawned. "How about we meet in a couple of hours?"

"I'm already at the farm," Jeremy informed me. "I got the call yesterday afternoon and decided to come to check it out. I thought I might be able to handle the workload on my own, but this is definitely a two-person job. Can you meet me here?"

The last thing I wanted to do was drive down the mountain when the dark clouds working their way over the summit hinted at snow that was likely to fall. Still, it had been my fault Jeremy had lost his only means of income. You see, I tend to be a bit of a buttinsky. In the past my meddling has caused a headache or two for the local sheriff, so when it became apparent that I was more than a little interested in the outcome of the murder investigation that was riveting the area over the Halloween weekend, my boss, County Commissioner Gordon Cromwell, warned me not to interfere. To make a long story short, I did, he fired me, and the local animal control facility where Jeremy and I worked was permanently closed.

"How exactly did you find out about this job?" I was still having a hard time believing that a simple farm job would pay the kind of money Jeremy was talking about.

"The estate executor called me. He must have seen one of the ads I posted. I really need a job, so I've got feelers out everywhere: Craigslist, Facebook, the local newspaper, fliers put up in all the businesses in the area. You name it, you'll find one of my ads."

"Okay. Text me the directions. I should be there in a few hours."

After I hung up my two dogs, Charlie and Maggie, adjusted their positions on the bed as I fell back into the soft cushion of my mattress. I turned onto my side and pulled a heavy comforter over my shoulders against the chilly alpine morning. What I really wanted to do was go back to sleep, but even I had to admit I'd turned into a bit of a slacker in the two weeks since I'd joined the ranks of the unwillingly unemployed. It sounded like Jeremy had been pounding the pavement looking for a new job while I had been happily wallowing in a cloak of self-pity worthy of the drama queen I tend to be. I supposed it was time to get back into some sort of regular routine, and a job, even a temporary one, might be the catalyst that would return me to the land of the living.

It wouldn't be so bad, I reasoned: a couple of weeks tending to a handful of cows, horses, and other livestock. I had a soft spot for cows, and the prospect of hanging out with the sweet-faced bovines held a certain appeal. My background included the care and rehabilitation of both wild and domestic animals, and while I'd never really worked with farm animals per se, I was certain Jeremy and I would be able to rise to the occasion.

I unfolded myself from the warm cocoon created by the mountain of blankets I slept under and stepped into my knee-high slippers. After pulling a warm sweatshirt over the long johns I wore to bed, I made my way down the stairs, tossed a fresh log on the smoldering fire, and started the coffee.

By the time I called my dad to ask him to check on my very pregnant rescue dog Maggie while Charlie and I met with Jeremy, the coffee had finished brewing. I poured a cup and walked out onto the deck overlooking the lake. I really do live in the ultimate spot. The boathouse, along with the fifty acres of lakefront property that goes with it, is owned by my maternal grandfather, who originally used it to house his boat. Nine years ago a group of farmers in the valley got together and challenged the legality of the Ashton Falls Dam, forcing its opening, which caused the water level to decrease dramatically. The boathouse now sits about twenty feet from the natural waterline. A few years ago I asked my mom if it would be possible to convert the abandoned structure and, surprisingly, my grandfather not only agreed but offered to pay for the renovation as well. Charlie and I have been living here ever since.

Charlie and Maggie chased each other on the beach as I sipped my beverage and watched a flock of geese fly in perfect formation over the glassy water of the nearby lake. The sun had just begun its daily ascent, bringing a scurry of activity to the forest floor. The mornings were getting colder as winter approached, and I knew that within a few weeks the mama bear and her cubs who visited every day would burrow into their den as the lazy days of summer gave way to the silence and serenity of a long, peaceful winter.

It was nearly eight thirty by the time I showered and dressed in warm clothing. After I said good-bye to Maggie, I called to Charlie, and headed out to the monster that would take me down the hill. You see, although I'm diminutive in size at a mere five foot tall, I drive a truck: a big one. A four-wheel drive, heavy-duty, extra-cab, lift-kit enhanced, long-bed monster. I find its size necessary, given the fact that I live and work in an environment where half of the miles I log each year are spent plowing through waist-deep snow or jolting along rutted dirt roads.

As I drove through town, I paused to look at the hundreds of thousands of twinkling lights that had appeared almost magically overnight. It was just two weeks until Thanksgiving and the official start of the holiday season. It looked like the proprietors of the town's shops were getting an early start on the decorating. In addition to the white globes that framed every window and doorway, there were lights hanging in every one of the small patio trees that lined the main drag. The gazebo in the town square was in the process of being decked out in anticipation of the giant tree that would be delivered and decorated the weekend after Thanksgiving. The first Friday in December was reserved for the annual tree lighting, and I knew that within the next couple of weeks there wouldn't be a store window left undecorated or a decorative lamppost without a wreath.

I love the excitement and enthusiasm that engulfs my little town as autumn morphs into winter. The smell of pumpkin mingled with cinnamon and nutmeg lingered as I passed Rosie's, the cafe my best friend, Ellie Davis, owns with her mother. Deciding that I had more than enough time for another cup of coffee, I pulled my truck to the side of the road and parked. I told Charlie to wait as I put on my jacket over my sweater and made my way toward the front of the building.

Rosie's is the quintessential alpine cafe, perched snuggly on the shoreline of Ashton Lake; it's surrounded by tall pines and quaking aspens that turn a brilliant yellow every autumn. On any given day, between the hours of six a.m. and two p.m., locals and visitors alike gather at Rosie's to share a meal and catch up on the latest gossip. Built on the north shore of the lake, Rosie's takes full advantage of the view with a wall of large windows nestled between knotty pine logs that make up the frame of the rugged, hand-milled cabin. The cafe is decorated with an eclectic assortment of skis, sleds, snowshoes, fishing poles, climbing ropes, and other antiques that define the area, while tables, both large and small, are arranged within the open and airy room around a huge floor-to-ceiling fireplace.

"Hey, Zoe, what are you doing out and about this early?" Ellie tucked a lock of her long brown hair behind her ear as she greeted me with her welcoming smile.

"I'm heading down the hill to see Jeremy about a temporary job," I replied. "I could smell the tantalizing aroma of your mom's muffins from the road. I've already eaten, but I couldn't resist."

"We have cranberry nut, pumpkin spice, caramel apple, lemon poppy seed, and chocolate cream," Ellie informed me.

"Caramel apple?"

"They're new," Ellie confirmed. "They're really good but also sort of messy. I'm thinking they're not the best choice for the road. If you want to take some to have with your coffee in the morning I'm sure you'll like them."

"Okay, give me a couple caramel apple muffins for later as well as a cranberry nut for the road. In fact, give me two cranberry nut muffins. Charlie is waiting in the truck. I'll take a coffee to go as well." I waved to the members of the local Rotary Club, who'd walked in and sat down in a booth overlooking the lake.

"Temporary job?" Ellie asked as I slid onto one of the bar stools lining the counter and she put the muffins into a bag with a handful of napkins.

"Something Jeremy found at one of the farms in the valley," I explained. "To be honest, I'm not thrilled about making the drive every day, but it's only for a couple of weeks at the most, and Jeremy sounded like he was in a bind."

"Maybe it won't be so bad. The trees are beautiful this time of year," Ellie pointed out as she filled my order. "That's one of the things I love about the foothills. The color lasts so much longer than it does up here on the mountain."

"That's true. You and I and Levi should get together this weekend. Maybe we can go for a drive through the valley like we have other years. We can stop at that old bar near the ski lodge and have a burger and a beer."

"Yeah, I'm in, but who knows about Levi with everything that's going on."

"Something's going on with Levi?"

"I just meant that with Barbie in the picture . . ."

Barbie, who by the way looks like the doll by the same name, is Levi's current girlfriend.

"Levi has dated dozens of women in the past and he never misses an opportunity to hang out with just the three of us," I reminded her. "Why should this be any different?"

"I don't know; there's just something about the whole Barbie thing that bugs me."

I had a feeling Ellie's discontent stemmed more from her changing feelings toward Levi than his current girlfriend, but I didn't say as much. Levi, Ellie and I have been friends for almost twenty years and during that time we've enjoyed an easy friendship free of the tangled emotions that accompany many relationships of the romantic kind. I've noticed lately, however, that Ellie's feelings toward Levi seem to be evolving.

"Barbie seems okay," I offered. "She's a bit over the top with her short skirts and tight sweaters, but Levi has dated worse."

"I know this is none of my business," Ellie continued, "and I probably shouldn't say anything, but Barbie came in for breakfast yesterday morning with that guy who runs the martial arts center."

"Barbie is a yoga instructor," I pointed out. "I'm sure that those in the fitness profession share a certain kinship."

"Maybe, but if you want my opinion, the woman is a bit too free in her associations. I'm afraid she's going to break Levi's heart."

"Levi's heart is made of titanium," I assured her. "If you want my opinion, he'll move on to someone new before the end of the month."

"Yeah, I guess you're right. It just bugs me the way Barbie flirts with everything in pants even when Levi is with her. I honestly don't know why he puts up with it."

"Levi is a big boy. He doesn't need you to protect him."

Ellie turned to look at the window behind her as Rosie set plates of Lumberjack Pancakes and creamy eggs benedict under the warmer. "I guess I should get back to work."

"Yeah, and I really should get going. I'll call you tonight so we can work out the details for the weekend," I suggested.

"Okay. Have a good day, and say hi to Jeremy for me."

"I will."

"Oh, and tell him that I have a pie for him. On the house," Ellie added.

"Pie?"

"He came in a couple of days ago looking for a piece of Mom's Pilgrim Pie but we were out, so I promised him a pie all to himself when Mom did the baking for the weekend. I've been holding one in the back since yesterday, but he never came by."

"He's already at the farm. I'll take the pie for him. I'm pretty sure he's planning to stay on-site if things work out."

Ellie boxed the pie as I nibbled on my muffin. Good thing I inherited my dad's stick-thin figure and überfast metabolism. Two breakfasts in one day was never really a good idea.

Ellie was right about the drive: the trip down the mountain *was* beautiful. A rambling river paralleled the narrow, winding road as the thick evergreen forest gave way to the colorful foothills still painted with autumn colors. I loved the sight of mule deer grazing in a meadow that had long since turned brown as the sun climbed into the sky. Once I'd fully awakened, I found that I was looking forward to my temporary career. I'd never worked on a farm before. The thought of lazy days spent among cows and chickens had a certain nostalgic appeal. My excitement grew with each passing mile, until I pulled onto the dirt drive associated with the address Jeremy had given me and got the shock of my life.

For those of you I have not yet met, my name is Zoe Donovan. I'm a twenty-four-year-old Pisces with a tendency to become overly involved in other people's problems and a propensity toward contradictory and erratic behavior. I have a big heart and an insatiable drive to rescue those in need. At times I bite off more than I can chew, creating a reality reminiscent of a bad dream, and this, apparently, is going to be a nightmare.

Chapter 2

A light snow was starting to fall as I climbed out of my truck and made my way over to the open area where Jeremy was waiting for me. I covered my nose against the stench as I stood ankle deep in turkey dung and surveyed the landscape before me. "How many are there?" I wondered as I viewed the sea of large birds crammed into pens much too small for the task.

"Several hundred at least," Jeremy answered. "I guess the birds were spread out over the property, but the estate executor had them rounded up and penned so they'd be easier to inventory and transport."

"Transport?" I hated to ask.

"For processing," Jeremy verified.

My stomach lurched at the mental image of exactly what *processing* would entail. Don't get me wrong: I'm an adult, and I do understand where Thanksgiving turkeys come from, but as a devoted animal rescue worker who has spent my entire career saving the lives of the animals in my care, the idea of babysitting a flock of birds scheduled for slaughter left an acidic taste in my mouth that I feared would linger long beyond my presence at the fowl-smelling property (pun intended).

"When you mentioned the job was at a farm, I was picturing cows and horses and maybe a few pigs," I accused.

"I know," Jeremy admitted. "I was afraid if I told you about the birds you wouldn't have come."

Jeremy was right. If he had told me the entire story, I probably wouldn't have come. While accepting this particular job goes against everything I believe in, it *had* been my fault that Jeremy lost his means of income, and if babysitting a few hundred turkeys for a couple of weeks would in any way make up for even a portion of the devastation I caused to his life, I guess I could put my feelings aside.

"Thanksgiving is in two weeks. The birds are scheduled for transport in ten days. If everything stays on schedule, we should be finished with the job by a week from Monday."

"Are you sure you want to do this?" I had to ask.

"It's not so much that I want to, but I really need the money," Jeremy answered. "I didn't want to mention it—it might have seemed like emotional blackmail, given the circumstances—but Gina just found out she's pregnant."

"Pregnant?"

Jeremy had only been dating the demanding model for a short time, and I was afraid it was way too early in their relationship to be dealing with something as life-altering as impending fatherhood. Besides, while I'll admit that most days I tend to be a bit lax about my appearance, Gina is a diva who cares more about her lip gloss than she does about the people around her. I never really understood why Jeremy was dating her in the first place.

"It was an accident." Jeremy blushed, a response I'd never before witnessed in the twenty-year-old heavy metal drummer, who sported a nose ring and a neck tattoo. "Gina doesn't want the baby. She wanted to end the pregnancy but finally agreed to go through with it if I would raise the baby and pay for all her expenses, up to and including any cost associated with returning her body back to supermodel status."

"I'm sorry," I said, taking Jeremy's hand. "You should have said something. I had no idea."

"With everything that's happened, I figured you had enough on your mind. I didn't want to concern you with my problems. Besides, I was embarrassed."

"Don't be." I smiled in an offer of support. "I admire what you're doing."

"I feel good about my decision. It's the right thing, but I need money, a lot of it. I've looked for other means of employment, but so far I haven't had any luck. Besides, I can earn as much with this short-term job as a regular gig would pay in two months. So about the job . . . ?"

"Okay," I reluctantly agreed.

"Thanks." He hugged me. "I know this position is the worst, but it's only for a couple of weeks at the most and I should make enough to pay this month's rent and give Gina some money."

"Are you and Gina still seeing each other?" I wondered.

"No, we broke up. Our relationship is strictly financial at this point."

I wasn't sorry to hear that Jeremy and Gina had parted ways. It would have been nice if Jeremy's baby had both a father and a mother, but Gina was as self-involved and flighty as anyone I'd ever met. No matter how hard I tried, I couldn't picture her as a mother, loving or otherwise.

"So when is the baby due?" I hoped Jeremy would have adequate time to get his financial situation worked out before taking on the task of single fatherhood.

"Not until the end of April, but Gina was quite adamant about my having enough money saved up to pay for whatever procedures she might require as soon as the baby's born. She has a contract for a shoot in Thailand in June."

"Gina is young," I said encouragingly. "Chances are her body will bounce back without an inordinate amount of coaxing as long as she watches her diet while she's expecting."

"Let's hope so. The spa she frequents when she needs to drop a few pounds costs almost a thousand dollars a day."

"Seriously?"

Jeremy shrugged. "You've seen her. Yes, she was blessed with enviable genetics, but she works hard for her body. I was actually surprised she was willing to go through with the pregnancy under any conditions. She's been really great, considering. If I want to be a father, I need to step up and make some money. I really feel like this gravy job is a sign that I'm doing the right thing."

"I don't suppose you know anything about the care and handling of turkeys?" Perhaps I should have asked this fairly obvious question before agreeing to this crazy idea.

"Not specifically," Jeremy admitted. "We've had birds at the shelter, and I have a contact who knows about the bigger birds. I suppose we can figure it out as we go along."

Terrific.

"I talked to Oliver, and he agreed to let you commute to the farm every day and go back home every evening if I agree to stay on-site," Jeremy informed me.

Jeremy had previously explained that Oliver Tisdale was the very unpleasant son of the recently deceased. While I wasn't looking forward to the daily commute, I much preferred returning to my boathouse up the mountain to staying on the property with hundreds of turkeys sentenced to death.

"We just need to go over to the house so you can fill out some paperwork," Jeremy said. "It won't take long, and then you can go. I can handle things today."

I took one final look at the beautiful birds whose days were numbered, then followed Jeremy. Based on the size of the two-story house, which was set apart from the weathered red buildings that housed the birds, I guessed there was money to be made in the raising and harvesting of the epicenter of the holiday meal. The home was laid out like a giant U with a double-wide entry in the center and a beautiful and peaceful garden with a large pool and a cascading waterfall in the rear. Jeremy led me through the double doors, which opened into a grand entry with a wide hallway in the center, as well as narrower hallways to the left and right.

"The main living area is straight ahead," Jeremy informed me. "We're supposed to meet in the library."

Charlie and I followed Jeremy down the hallway to the left. There were windows overlooking the farm and colorful foothills on the right, with closed doors on the left. The library was an impressive room, with dark paneling, hand-carved moldings, a cozy fireplace, an inviting seating area, and hundreds of books lined on hardwood shelves. It was connected by an open door to a large, office-type conference room in which eight people were sitting around a long, rectangular table, arguing about who was and who was not worthy of a portion of the proverbial pie.

"I guess we'll have to wait for them to finish," Jeremy whispered, as we peered through the window separating the library from the conference room.

"So those are the heirs?" I asked.

"Afraid so." Jeremy took a seat next to me from which we could observe the circus from a distance. "I have to say they're an interesting group."

"You've met them?"

"A few."

"So fill me in." I couldn't help but be curious about the eclectic group who, based on the argument I'd witnessed thus far, appeared to be coldhearted leeches.

"The older gentleman at the head of the table is Mason Perot, the late Charles Tisdale's attorney," Jeremy said. "Like I mentioned before, he's drawn up a fairly specific contract as to our duties and compensation that you'll need to sign before you leave."

The attorney was a diminutive man of portly stature. He was an odd-looking fellow with a perfectly smooth, bald head and round glasses that covered protruding eyes. It occurred to me that he looked a bit like Mr. Magoo of the classic cartoons I'd watched as a child. I hoped he wasn't as dim-witted as his cartoon look-alike or this was going to be a very lengthy negotiation.

"To his right is the man who first contacted me, estate executor and Charles's eldest son, Oliver Tisdale," Jeremy continued.

Oliver reminded me of a crane or some other gangly bird. His eyes were cold and his countenance controlled as he studied the other people seated around the table while they argued over who should and should not be privy to the substantial estate. His intense stare and lifeless expression gave me a chill that worked its way up my spine and then settled at the base of my throat.

"Who's the woman to Oliver's right?" I asked.

"His wife, Olivia."

"Oliver and Olivia?" I giggled. "Really?"

"'Fraid so."

Olivia, like Oliver, was tall and regal, with dark hair and dark eyes. Both were thin to the point of gauntness and presented an air of controlled sophistication that didn't quite jibe with the expensive but faded clothes they wore. If I had to guess, I'd say they'd had a substantial amount of money at some point.

Jeremy continued to identify the occupants of the room as I studied each in turn. Sitting across from Oliver, to Mason's left, was a portly man with chubby cheeks and a round head. He was as bald as he was rotund and looked freakishly similar to Uncle Fester from *The Addams Family* movie. Jeremy informed me that he was the second eldest son of the recently deceased: Leroy Tisdale. Based on the redness of his fleshy face and the beads of sweat on his brow, it appeared that, unlike his quiet and controlled brother, he had a temper and wasn't afraid to show it.

"And the woman to Leroy's left?" I inquired.

"His sister and Charles's only daughter, Peggy."

Peggy, like Leroy, was a bit on the plump side, with a reddish skin tone and thinning blond hair that was held together with at least a can of hairspray. I cringed at the bright blue eye shadow and red blush on her fleshy cheeks, which gave her a clown-like appearance.

"To Peggy's left is her daughter, Margaret," Jeremy continued.

Margaret had shoulder-length blond hair and a nice smile. She was a bit on the plain side, but, unlike her gaudily dressed mother, she wore little makeup and was dressed in an appropriate black dress.

"At the end of the table, opposite Mason, is Charles's grandson Brent, who, like Charles's children, Oliver, Leroy, and Peggy, is a beneficiary. He is the son of Charles's youngest child, Bertram, who is currently incarcerated and so not in attendance."

I looked at the man Jeremy was referring to. He was handsome, in his early twenties, with thick brown hair, dark eyes, and a bored expression on his face. Of all the members of the family, he looked to be the least interested in defending whatever tidbit the old man had left him. I noticed that he winked at the woman to his left, a strikingly beautiful brunette, as Leroy launched into a tirade worthy of a spoiled child.

"And the girl sitting to Brent's left?" I wondered.

"Her name is Holly. Apparently, she's the daughter of Charles's mistress, Dolly Robinson, who isn't in attendance. Interestingly enough, she inherited a portion of the estate equal to the other members of the family."

"How do you know all of this?" I wondered.

"When I arrived yesterday I was curious about the family, so I struck up a conversation with Mason's intern, a very helpful and informed woman who was at loose ends while Mason met with Oliver behind closed doors."

"So you felt it was the polite thing to do to keep her entertained?"

"Exactly."

"And where is this intern today?"

"I'm not sure. Unfortunately Mason came alone."

"Let me guess," I teased. "Mason's intern happens to be young and beautiful."

Jeremy grinned. The guy had a type, and if the intern was blond and stacked I had no doubt he'd talked to her for quite some time.

"Okay, let me see if I've got this straight." I studied the interesting group. "Oliver is Charles's eldest son. He's both an heir and the estate executor. He's married to Olivia, who isn't a beneficiary. Charles's second son, Leroy, also an heir, is here alone. His sister, Peggy, who's mentioned in the will as well, is here with her daughter, Margaret, who was not named a beneficiary."

"So far, so good." Jeremy chuckled at my attempt to make sense of this circus.

"Charles's grandson Brent is both a beneficiary and in attendance. His father Bertram is in prison and not in attendance. Do you know what he's in prison for?"

"Manslaughter."

"Do you know who he killed?"

"No, I didn't think to ask."

I glanced back toward the table. The arguing had ceased and everyone was sitting around staring at one another as they waited to see who would make the next move. The woman sitting on Brent's left leaned in toward him and whispered something in his ear. "And last but not least, the final participant in this little game," I continued as I watched the woman, "is the young and beautiful Holly, who is an heir even though she's in no way related to the others and is in fact the daughter of Charles's mistress, Dolly."

"Bingo."

"Do we know why Dolly isn't in attendance?"

"*We* don't," Jeremy teased.

"Okay, then do *you* know why Dolly isn't in attendance?"

"I don't. She hasn't been here since I've been on the property. She's evidently not named in the will, so she may feel there isn't a reason for her presence."

"If she was currently 'dating'"—I used the term loosely—"Charles at the time of his death, you'd think she'd be here to see to the final arrangements."

Jeremy shrugged. "You'd think. Maybe she's mad that she wasn't included in the money grab."

"Maybe. Are there any heirs not in attendance?" I wondered.

"I don't know."

I continued to study the strange group at the table. "It's odd that Oliver looks so much different from either Leroy or Peggy, who do share a family resemblance."

"Different mothers," Jeremy explained.

"How long exactly did you talk with this intern?"

"A while." Jeremy blushed. "Although it was the neighbor, Pike, who filled me in on the wives."

"When did you have time to speak to the neighbor?"

"When I first arrived, Mason suggested that I speak to the man. He assured me that Charles and Pike had been close friends for years, and if there was anything specific I needed to know about the turkeys, he'd be the best source of that information. It was a worthwhile conversation on many levels."

"Why is that?"

"For one thing, the man loves to talk. Not only did he give me some tips on caring for the birds but he was able to elaborate on the heirs and other guests as well. I guess he was Charles's best friend and has known the family since Charles bought the property when Oliver was four."

"So what did he tell you about the wives?"

"It seems Oliver is the child of Charles's first wife, Amelia, who died in her sleep when Oliver was six. Leroy and Peggy were born to wife number two, Penelope, whom Charles divorced shortly after Peggy's birth. Brent's father, Bertram, was born out of wedlock to a prostitute by the name of Lola, who later married Charles and lived with him for almost twenty years until Charles hooked up with Dolly. Lola now lives in Los Angeles."

"This sounds like a soap opera." I giggled.

"It gets better," Jeremy assured me. "Pike seems convinced that Charles was murdered, and that one of the people sitting at that table is the one who killed him. According to the man, each and every one of the guests currently staying at the estate has a reason for wanting the man dead."

"Charles was murdered? I thought I heard that he fell and hit his head."

"The official story at this point is that Charles had an accident, but Pike seems certain that there is more going on. When I spoke to him, he insisted that his old friend had been murdered."

"Okay, say he's right and Charles was murdered. You said the guests all have motives for killing the man. What kind of motives?" I had to admit I was curious.

"For a start, Oliver has reason to believe that his father killed his mother. At the time of Amelia's death, there was speculation that she was slowly being poisoned because the autopsy revealed there was belladonna in her system. Charles claimed his wife dabbled in herbal remedies to deal with the various ailments from which she suffered most of her life. He claimed that if it was the belladonna that killed her, it was by her own hand. This statement could be neither proven nor disproven, so Charles was never charged with her death, although Pike said that many of the neighbors in the area felt that Charles was a cold and uncaring man who could easily have killed his sickly wife rather than deal with the enormous expense and workload her frail state generated."

"What did Pike think?"

"He believed Charles when he insisted that he was innocent, but he did admit that there were a lot of unanswered questions surrounding the woman's death."

"I can see how that gives Oliver a reason to want his father dead, but why kill him now? It's been years."

"According to Pike, Oliver was just a child when his mother died and therefore most likely unaware of what was going on. Pike told me that after the police dropped the investigation, Charles met Penelope, and the whole sordid affair was swept under the rug. Two years ago, Oliver and Olivia were involved in an investment scam that resulted in the loss of their home and most of their worldly possessions to bankruptcy. Oliver asked Charles for money but was turned down. Charles felt that a man needed to make his own way."

"So how does this tie in with Amelia's death?" I wondered.

"Olivia, apparently, wasn't going to take no for an answer, so she started digging around in Charles's past. She figured if she could find some dirt on him, she could use that as leverage to get the money they needed. During her search she found information about the investigation of Amelia's death and tried to blackmail Charles."

"Did it work? Did Charles give them the money they needed?"

"No. He told them that their failures weren't his problem and they needed to figure out their financial mess themselves. According to Pike, Charles threatened to cut Oliver out of his will but never did."

"So Oliver just recently found out that his father might have killed his mother, giving him a motive, and Olivia wanted Charles's money to restore her lifestyle and might have found out about the potential change in the will, giving her a motive as well."

"Exactly."

"And the others?"

"It seems that Leroy grew up with the assumption that he'd one day take over for his father, because Oliver showed no interest in the turkeys or the farm. According to Pike, Leroy worked hard for his father for most of his adult life, only to be told by Charles a few years ago that he didn't intend to leave him the farm as Leroy believed but rather planned to instruct Oliver as estate executor to sell the property upon his death. Leroy was angry, quit his job, and immediately left the property, but according to Pike, Leroy contacted Charles a couple of months ago in an attempt to have him reconsider his position."

"And did he? Reconsider?"

"Pike says no. He said that Leroy was furious and insisted that Charles owed him for all his years of labor."

"Okay, so Leroy was angry at his father, which I guess gives him motive as well. If he decided to confront him in person, he could have killed him in a fit of rage. What about the others?"

"Peggy and her father have been on the outs for years. Pike told me that Charles disinherited Peggy when she married a man her father considered to be beneath his station in life. Peggy hadn't had any contact with her father since she left home at the age of eighteen until she contacted him three months ago."

"Why did she contact him after all those years?"

"Margaret needs surgery to repair a genetic heart defect. It's not life threatening at this point, but if left unattended it could lead to premature heart disease. Margaret's physician strongly recommended that the matter be attended to sooner rather than later in order to avoid complications. Peggy wrote to her father and asked for the money. Pike said that Charles showed him the letter, which in his opinion was both open and heartfelt. She not only explained why she needed the money but apologized for defying him and confessed that she regretted not having him in her life for all those years. He never responded to her."

"Wow, that's cold."

"Pike told me that he tried to convince Charles to give Peggy the money she needed, but when he made his case on Peggy's behalf, Charles simply said, 'Peggy who?'"

"What a jerk." I couldn't believe anyone would treat his family quite so horribly, no matter what they'd done. "I hate to even say this, but it sounds like a hell of a motive for murder to me. So what about Brent and Holly?"

"Brent grew up in a dysfunctional family where both parents drank heavily. He often spent summers at the turkey farm with his grandparents. While he tended to butt heads with Charles, he adored Lola. According to Pike, Lola actually loved Charles and was devastated when he tossed her aside for the young and beautiful Dolly. Brent resented his grandfather for what he did to his grandmother and distanced himself accordingly, but for some reason, to which Pike was not privy, Brent came to see Charles a week ago. Pike said that Brent's visit greatly upset Charles, but he refused to talk to him about the encounter, so he doesn't know exactly what occurred. Pike did say that Charles wasn't easily ruffled and Brent's visit left him solemn and agitated, so the discussion they shared must have been significant."

"And Holly?"

"In Pike's opinion Holly probably has the least motive of any of the visitors to want Charles dead, but Pike did say that she often complained to Charles about the callous way he treated her mother."

"He wasn't kind to his mistress?"

"Pike says no."

"Do you think it's odd that Pike would befriend a heartless man like Charles for all of those years?" I asked.

"I did at first, but Pike was pretty upfront about the fact that as a family member Charles was a brute, but as a neighbor he was a pretty good guy who was always willing to lend a hand. He said that Charles came through for him on more than one occasion."

"Weird." Suddenly this gruesome job was becoming slightly more interesting. It wouldn't be so bad babysitting a bunch of turkeys in preparation for slaughter if I could indulge my natural inclination to snoop by looking into Charles's untimely death as long as I was here. A dead body, seven likely suspects; what could be better?

Chapter 3

After Mason was freed up to help us with the paperwork I needed to sign, I made my way back to my truck. Upon returning to the boathouse, I took off my muddy shoes, lit the fire I'd built that morning in my river-rock fireplace, fed Maggie and my cats Marlow and Spade, then headed into the bathroom to give Charlie a vigorous bath. It took three sudsings before I managed to wash the stench of the turkey farm out of his long, tan coat, but by the time I was finished he more closely resembled the cuddly bundle of fur I knew and loved. I decided that, as much as I loved bringing Charlie to work, perhaps a turkey farm wasn't the best place for the little dog.

After drying Charlie and refilling everyone's food and water, I took a shower and changed into a comfortable pair of sweatpants and an overly large yet snuggly sweatshirt. Deciding to leave my long, curly hair to its own devices, I made a peanut butter sandwich, poured a glass of milk, and settled onto the overstuffed sofa in front of the fireplace. I thought about Jeremy's situation as I ate my dinner.

I have a soft spot for dads who step up and raise their kids when their mothers don't want them. I myself am the by-product of my wealthy mother's single act of teenage rebellion with my locally beloved yet financially lacking, blue-collar father. When my uptight and stodgy grandparents found out that my mother was pregnant, they shipped her off to an "aunt's," where I, under the shroud of absolute secrecy, was delivered into the world. My grandparents wanted an anonymous adoption, but my dad fought hard and convinced them that he would raise me in isolation from the judgmental eyes of their upper-class friends. Jeremy is young but, like my dad, he is kind and responsible and will make a great father. The more I think about it, the more I'm convinced that I've made the right choice in agreeing to take this crazy job.

I glanced at the phone and considered calling my dad. I'd recently found out that he'd been in contact with my mother and had failed to mention it to me, even though I saw him on almost a daily basis. I'd made the decision a few weeks ago to let him tell me in his own time, but he'd had plenty of opportunities and so far had failed to do so. I supposed if I really wanted to know what was going on, I was going to need to bring up the subject myself.

I reached for the phone as Charlie leaped up from the sofa, where he'd been sleeping, and ran to the door. He began hopping and dancing around in a way that indicated he already knew our new neighbor had stopped by for a visit. I opened the door and smiled as my ex-nemesis, Zak Zimmerman, strolled up the front walkway with his chocolate lab, Lambda. For reasons unknown to me, Charlie loves Zak. I mean, he really loves him. When Levi and Ellie stop by, he's always happy to see them, but if Zak is anywhere near the boathouse, Charlie starts jumping around in a joyful display I've come to think of as his happy dance.

"I'm glad you stopped by," I greeted as Zak brushed snow from his shoulders.

"You are?" Zak looked surprised, and I didn't really blame him. You see, for years I considered Zak to be my archenemy. Our relationship began in the seventh grade, when he beat me in the mathathon for which I'd been studying relentlessly for almost three months. The worst part of it was, I'd invited my maternal grandparents, a scary couple I'd met only a handful of times yet still inexplicably wanted to please, and, miracle of miracles, this untouchable couple, who valued achievement above all else, actually had agreed to come. Following what I still in many ways consider my biggest defeat came six years of second-place finishes to Zak's first for every science fair, spelling bee, and academic competition I entered until we both graduated high school.

"I am." I hate to admit it, but I've been a total bitch to Zak, even though he's never been anything but super nice to me. Everyone I know seems to love the guy, and I have to admit that during the horror of the past few weeks he's been there for me like nobody else.

Zak greeted Charlie, kissed me on the cheek, and walked through the front door of my tiny yet awesome home.

"Care for a PB&J?" I offered.

"I brought wine."

For the first time I noticed the bottle he carried.

"Even better." I took the wine into the kitchen and opened it.

"When I talked to you earlier you mentioned that you were on your way to check out a job in the valley. How'd it go?"

"Okay, I guess. On the minus side, I have to spend the next two weeks caring for a bunch of birds I already know are going to end up on the chopping block. The entire notion makes me sick to my stomach. On the plus side, it looks like there might be a really complex murder mystery to keep me distracted."

"Murder mystery?" Zak accepted the glass of wine I offered him and returned to the living room.

"Okay," I geared up, "get this."

I guess it's sort of morbid for someone who values life to the extent I do to get all worked up when there's a murder to solve, but I'd like to go on record at this point to remind you all that I often display random and contradictory behavioral responses that no one, including myself, can ever really explain.

"The owner of the turkey farm died two days ago under what can only be described as unusual and mysterious circumstances. The farmer from the neighboring property showed up to share a cup of coffee and found Charles Tisdale dead on the kitchen floor. He called the police, who have yet to release an official cause of death, but the neighbor, who goes by the name of Pike, told Jeremy that it looked like Charles had been hit over the head."

I took a deep breath before continuing. "Jeremy mentioned this to Charles Tisdale's attorney, Mason Perot, who claimed that Charles wasn't murdered but merely fell and hit his head on the corner of the kitchen table."

"And why are you so certain this attorney is lying?" Zak asked.

I shrugged. "Because it makes a better story if Charles was murdered, and I could use a distraction from the saga of birds on death row."

Zak grinned. "Makes sense. Go on."

"Anyway, shortly after Jeremy arrived at the farm, a whole herd of relatives showed up. Honestly, if I was going to make this story up, I couldn't have come up with a better cast of characters."

"Ah, the suspects," Zak correctly deduced.

"It's sort of complicated," I warned. "You might want to write this down."

"I have a good memory. Go on," Zak encouraged.

I spent the next several minutes explaining everything I'd learned from Jeremy.

"Okay, let me get this straight," Zak repeated. "Charles has four children: Oliver, Leroy, Peggy, and Bertram. Oliver is at the farm with his wife, Olivia, Leroy arrived alone, and Peggy is in attendance with her daughter, Margaret. Bertram is in jail."

"Yes," I confirmed. "But Bertram's son, Brent, is a participant in the discussion and, apparently, an heir to the estate."

"Maybe Brent is simply getting his dad's share," Zak guessed.

"Yeah, that's what I think, too, but I've yet to confirm that."

"So is that it?"

"No. The most interesting heir of all is Holly, the daughter of the mistress Charles was keeping time with right up until he died. According to Jeremy, Holly is going to receive a portion equal to Oliver, Leroy, Peggy, and Brent's."

"And Holly's mother?" Zak wondered.

"I'm not sure. Her name is Dolly, but as of this afternoon she hadn't been on the property and Jeremy hadn't met her. Still, I suppose we should find out."

"We?"

"You are going to help me?" I asked. "With the murder, not the turkeys."

"Do you want me to?"

I was surprised, but I did. I nodded.

"Okay, I'm in."

I hugged Zak. It was a new and strange experience to have warm and fuzzy feelings for a man I once loathed. I wasn't sure if my feelings for my former nemesis stemmed more from the temporary insanity I'd been experiencing since being fired from the job that meant more to me than I can express or my willingness to open my eyes and see the man everyone else has been in love with for quite some time.

"So where do we start?"

"I suppose we should verify that Charles Tisdale actually was murdered," Zak suggested. "If his injury was the result of a slip and fall, as the attorney suggested, this entire enterprise may be futile at best."

"So how do we find out the results of the autopsy?"

"Do you have a computer?"

"Yeah, hang on, I'll get it."

As I climbed the stairs to the loft that serves as my bedroom, I could hear Zak talking to the dogs. I don't know why I'd never noticed how kind and gentle he could be. It's odd spending a lifetime hating someone for being so much better at everything than you are, only to find out they're also one of the nicest and most genuine people on the planet. I had a hard time letting go of my resentment toward Zak, but once I did, I was afraid I might have opened the gate to emotions I'm fairly certain I'm not yet ready to deal with.

"It's kind of old," I warned him as I handed him my five-year-old laptop. I was embarrassed by my meager attempt at living in the age of information and social networking. Zak is a genius. And not just an average genius, but a freaking full-on computer nerd who built his own software company in his garage during his formative years and then sold it to Microsoft for tens of millions of dollars when he turned twenty-one.

I watched as Zak's large hands manipulated the keyboard in a masterful way I'd never been able to pull off. Now that I've slowly begun to remove the blinders where Zak is concerned, I can see that my former enemy is actually a remarkably handsome man. Freakishly tall with broad shoulders and sandy blond hair that brushes his shoulders. He has blue eyes that are framed by impossibly long lashes that graze his bushy but well-shaped eyebrows. I guess I've always known that Zak is handsome, but I've only recently been able to look into his eyes and see the depth of intelligence and compassion that others have recognized for years.

"It looks like the official medical examiner's report suggests that Charles was hit over the head with a blunt object, most likely rectangular in shape. The wound was inconsistent with his hitting his head on the table near where he was found."

"They have that information right there on the Web?" I asked.

"Sure, if you have the ability to hack into the police database." Zak grinned.

"You hacked in?"

"You wanted to know what was on the report."

"Yeah, but I don't want you to end up in jail."

"You know," Zak said, "I think that's the nicest thing you've ever said to me."

I blushed. I really have been a bitch to him.

"Don't worry. I know what I'm doing. I was in and out before anyone even knew I was there."

"Okay, so we know Charles was killed. Now we just need to figure out by whom, with what, and why."

"Before we go any further, I need to ask once more, why are we doing this?"

"Dead turkeys," I explained. "Lots and lots of almost-dead turkeys. I need a distraction, and a murder investigation is a good distraction from all the death and mayhem."

"Did anyone ever tell you you're a little peculiar?"

"Every damn day." I smiled.

"Let's make a list and see where it leads us," Zak suggested. "Any chance we can get into Charles's private spaces: his office, for a start?"

I wasn't sure. Jeremy was staying out there, so we could always enlist his help, but the house was full of dueling heirs, each one suspicious of the others. Chances are they'd be keeping an eye on one another, as well as everyone else.

"Maybe," I finally answered. "We can try. For now, let's just write down everything we know, as well as what we need to find out."

"If we count everyone staying at the farm we have Oliver, Olivia, Leroy, Peggy, Margaret, Brent, and Holly," Zak listed. "That gives us seven plus the attorney Mason, which bring us to eight."

"Correct."

"Okay, I added all seven visitors as well as Mason to the list." Zak typed the names into the computer database. "I suppose we should look at those who weren't there."

I frowned as I tried to sort out what Zak meant.

"Any children Oliver and Olivia may have, Leroy's wife, Peggy's husband, Holly's mother, Brent's mother, all the ex-wives."

I thought about it. "Oliver's mother, Amelia, is dead. Leroy and Peggy's mother, Penelope, was divorced by Charles and may hold a grudge. I don't know where she is or what happened to her, but we should add her to the list. Bertram's mother, Lola, divorced Charles when he hooked up with Dolly. Someone mentioned that Lola is living in Los Angeles, but I don't know anything about Dolly. I guess we should add them to the list. No one mentioned Leroy's wife or Peggy's husband, but I suppose we should check them out."

"You said that Brent's dad is in jail, but how about his mom?" Zak wondered.

"Never mentioned."

"Okay, this is what I have so far. Charles has four children, Oliver, Leroy, Peggy, and Bertram," Zak read. "Bertram is in jail, so he has an alibi."

"Okay, so that gives us three suspects," I confirmed. "Brent, Olivia, Margaret, and Holly are also on-site, bringing the total number of suspects to seven."

"If you add in the attorney that gives us eight," Zak added. "If we count Peggy's husband, Leroy's wife, and Bertram's wife, that brings us to eleven."

"And then we have all the ex-wives and lovers," I added. "We know that Amelia is dead, so we have Penelope, Lola, and Dolly, bringing the total up to fourteen. Fourteen is a lot."

"Yeah, but I'm betting if we look at proximity, we'll be able to eliminate a few. My hunch is that by the end of the day tomorrow we'll have whittled the list down to a couple of names. The other possibility is that none of these people are guilty of the murder and an as-yet-unnamed individual is the culprit."

"It's late. I should get some sleep. Can you come with me to the farm in the morning?" I asked.

"What time should I be here?"

"Eight?"

"Eight it is. I'll bring breakfast."

Chapter 4

The next morning I called Ellie and asked if she could stop by to check on Maggie. She's due to deliver her puppies any day now, and I worry about her ability to do so unaided because she was severely malnourished when I first got her. For the same reason, I'm also worried about the health of the puppies she carries. Although Maggie has only been with me for a couple of weeks, I love her more than I can say. She is a resilient survivor who is a sweet and loving dog in spite of the fact that the puppy-mill owner we rescued her from both starved and abused her.

"Thanks for coming," I greeted Ellie when she showed up at my door at seven thirty.

"No problem," Ellie stated as she bent down to pet Charlie and Maggie, who had rushed to the door to greet her. "The restaurant is slow today, so it isn't a problem for me to take some time off. I was actually thinking about just hanging out here, if that's okay. I have a book I've been dying to get to, and with your view plus the cozy fire, it seems like a perfect place to read it."

"That's more than okay, that's perfect." I was relieved that someone would be here with Maggie.

"I love to watch the storms sneak in over the summit," Ellie commented as she looked out one of the picture windows facing the lake. "Those dark clouds with the flurries of snow that hint at winter just around the corner always make me anxious for snowboard season."

"I heard we're in for more than flurries by next week," I informed her as I threw a couple of logs on the fire.

"My snowboard is all serviced and ready to go." Ellie helped herself to a cup of coffee. "I can't wait to try out the new runs they built on Piney Mountain over the summer. One of the ski-lodge owners came into the restaurant a few days ago. He told me that the black diamond run is going to be the most challenging one they've ever had."

"I can't wait to try it. The old runs are getting boring. I'd planned to get a new board this year, but with my recent unemployment . . ."

"Your old board is two years newer than my new board," Ellie pointed out.

"True," I admitted. I love to snowboard and have a tendency to buy a new board every year or two. "There's plenty of food in the fridge," I informed her. "Help yourself to whatever. I'll be home around six, if you want to hang out until then. We can make some dinner and watch it snow."

"Sounds perfect. I'll see if Levi wants to join us. He came into Rosie's yesterday and he mentioned that Barbie was out of town for the weekend. He's on for a drive this weekend as well."

"Yeah, about the drive, it looks like I'll be tied up on the turkey farm every day until after the birds are shipped for processing, but dinner sounds good. I'll ask Zak to stay for dinner as well. He's giving up his time to help me today."

"I'll make some fettuccini," Ellie offered. "I've been in the mood for a good carb orgy."

"Sounds perfect. There's stuff for salad in the crisper and wine in the rack. Thanks again for doing this."

"Thanks for letting me hang out here. I'm really looking forward to some peace and quiet. It's been a while since I've had time to reflect, and maybe take a nap."

"There are a couple of quilts in that trunk if you decide to go for the nap while I'm floundering around with the turkeys." I nodded toward the old captain's trunk I use as a coffee table.

"I still can't believe you took this crazy assignment." Ellie laughed.

"I'm doing it for Jeremy."

"He still can't find a job?"

"No." I shook my head. "He isn't having any better luck than I am, in spite of the fact that he's been looking a lot harder."

"But a turkey farm? The guy is collecting unemployment. I honestly can't see him being desperate enough to even consider such a gruesome undertaking. I don't see how you're going to be able to look those turkeys in the eye, knowing that in a few days' time they're going to be missing their heads."

"Believe me, I'm not looking forward to spending almost two weeks with turkeys on death row, but Jeremy has incurred some unexpected expenses and I feel like I owe him. After all, it's my fault he's in this predicament in the first place."

"He lose his shirt gambling again?" Ellie guessed. Jeremy is a great guy, but he does love his poker.

"Actually, his financial issues have more to do with parenting than gambling."

"Come again?"

"I'm not sure I'm supposed to tell anyone this, but Jeremy didn't specifically say not to. Gina recently found out she's expecting. The baby is due in April, and Jeremy has agreed to pay all related expenses."

"Wow. Poor Jeremy. Are they getting married?"

"No. He's going to raise the baby on his own."

"Geez. I guess I can see why you're willing to go to such lengths to help him. If you need anything, let me know. I'd like to do what I can to help him out."

"I'm sure he'll appreciate that. For now, maybe just don't say anything. Like I said, I'm not sure if the word is out or if Jeremy and Gina are trying to keep it a secret for the time being."

"No problem. I won't say a thing. I know it's early, but you should tell Jeremy to talk to Rick." Rick is the man Ellie had been dating. "His brother Rob's girlfriend recently had a baby and after much consideration, Rob decided to raise the baby rather than give it up for adoption. Rick said Rob felt like he was in over his head, so he started a support group for single parents. They trade babysitting and that sort of thing."

"That sounds like a good connection for Jeremy. I'll tell him. Speaking of Rick," I said, using the opening provided, "I haven't seen him around lately. Are you two still dating?"

"No." Ellie looked away. "We're still friends, but we've pretty much decided that we weren't a really great couple."

"That's too bad. Rick is a good guy."

"He is, but we just didn't click the way . . ." Ellie hesitated. I was waiting for her to say *Levi and I do*, but she never did. "The way we should," she finished.

"Yeah, I get it. Zak should be here any minute. I guess I'll go grab my coat and stuff. Call me if anything comes up."

"Your cell on?"

I looked. It wasn't. I'm not sure why turning the darn thing on is such a challenge for me.

"Yeah." I pushed the power button. "It's on. If Maggie goes into labor and you can't get hold of me, call Scott." Scott Walden is the veterinarian I worked with at the shelter up until a few weeks ago. "I left Scott's number on the notepad on the front of the refrigerator."

"Don't worry, we'll be fine," Ellie assured me. "I hear turkeys are dumb birds. I hope they don't give you any trouble."

"Trouble? How much trouble can a few hundred birds be?"

If only I knew.

Chapter 5

As promised, Zak showed up with Lambda in tow at exactly eight o'clock. I explained that the turkey farm wasn't really a good place for a dog, and Lambda was happy to hang with Ellie, Charlie, and Maggie. We ate our breakfast sandwiches on the road and showed up at Charles Tisdale's farm by eight forty-five, fifteen minutes before the agreed-upon time of nine o'clock. Zak and I decided to pretend he was interested in buying the farm, which the heirs had made known they were very interested in selling. This gave him a plausible reason to hang around and ask questions.

Jeremy and I spent the first several hours feeding the large birds and then herding them from pen to pen as we cleaned the open pens behind them. We checked each bird for any nicks, abrasions, or other health issues before sorting them into those with clean bills of health and those that might need a closer look. By the time all the birds were fed and cared for and all the pens cleaned, it was well into the afternoon. At this rate I had no idea how I was going to have any time to investigate Charles Tisdale's murder, but Jeremy volunteered to tend to the sick and injured birds while I helped Zak snoop around.

"Remind me to bring clean clothes to change into tomorrow." I grimaced at the smell I knew was coming from my person. I dusted off my clothes the best I could, removed my shoes, and entered the house. As luck would have it, there was a viewing scheduled at the mortuary that afternoon, so everyone would be gone for at least another hour.

"What you really need is coveralls to protect your clothes, and shoes you can burn after your time here is over," Zak suggested. "Any idea where the office is?"

"Yeah, I was there yesterday. Follow me." I led Zak to the office where I had signed the paperwork the previous day. Zak set his laptop on the coffee table while I began looking around. "What are we looking for?" I asked.

"I don't know," Zak admitted. "Maybe a will or some other type of legal document. Correspondence could provide useful information as well. After I got home last night, I whittled down our list from fourteen to eight."

"Eight is better." I was impressed. "What did you find out?"

"Leroy is a lifelong bachelor, so we can eliminate his wife as a suspect. Penelope moved to Florida after divorcing Charles, remarried, and still lives there."

"That brings us to twelve," I subtracted.

"Peggy's husband was killed in an automobile accident six years ago, and Bertram's ex-wife and Brent's mother is the reason Bertram is in jail for manslaughter."

"He killed her?"

"He forced her into a vehicle while under the influence of drugs and alcohol and then ran his car off the road. It was undetermined whether the accident was intentional, but she died, and Bertram was charged with manslaughter and is currently serving his sentence."

"Wow, poor Brent. Okay, so now there are ten."

"Lola moved to Los Angeles after divorcing Charles, and I've confirmed that she was at work on the day of Charles's murder. Holly lives in Portland and just arrived here yesterday after hearing about Charles's death from her mother, Dolly, who apparently keeps her own apartment. Holly is staying there rather than at the house during this process."

"And Dolly's alibi?"

"I haven't been able to contact her. I eliminated Holly from the list, but not Dolly."

"So where does that leave us?"

"Mason Perot has been Charles's attorney for more than ten years. He lives in the area and I haven't yet been able to confirm an alibi for him. We know he's either lying or misleading people as to the cause of death, so in my mind he stays at the top of the list."

"And Oliver and Olivia? Do we know where they live?"

"Bryton Lake. And Leroy, Peggy, Margaret, and Brent are still on the list as well," Zak confirmed.

I pried open the top drawer of the desk and began sorting through mail, which looked to have been delivered over the past month. Mostly bills, many unpaid, but there was one envelope that caught my attention. I pulled the legal-size document from the envelope and began to read.

"I noticed you had a long discussion with Mason while Jeremy and I were working with the birds. Did you discover anything relevant?" I asked.

"As a prospective buyer, I asked to see financial statements and employee files. I did some digging and found out that Charles Tisdale is worth upward of fifty million dollars."

"Did you say fifty?" I gasped. "Why in the hell is someone with fifty million dollars working a turkey farm?"

"Apparently he liked turkeys," Zak informed me. "I spoke to Margaret earlier, and she said her grandfather hadn't always been rich. In fact, he grew up quite poor. He took out a loan to buy the land where the farm now sits. Charles inherited a load of money from a grandfather he barely knew before Margaret was born. Although Margaret never met her grandfather, she shared that according to her mother, Charles clawed his way from poverty and developed a stringent work ethic as a young man. It was very important to him that people work for and earn what they have. He hadn't felt he'd earned the money he inherited, so he didn't really want it. He hasn't touched a single penny of it in all the years he's had it. Never spent it; never invested it. It's just sitting in a bank collecting one-percent interest."

"Do you find that odd?" I asked.

"I did, but what's even odder is the lack of employees. Even if the guy loved turkeys, you'd think he'd hire someone to do the dirty work. I searched the records and found that prior to a week ago, the farm had five staff," Zak said, "a farm manager named Bill Parker and four assistants who worked part- time. Bill and the others were promised a percentage of the profit from the sale of the birds in exchange for a reduction in pay. The problem is, Charles laid everyone off a week before he died."

"Charles was going to rip them off," I decided. "The guy had fifty million dollars. What exactly was his deal?"

"That I don't know. What I do know is that the former employees hired an attorney who was going to sue Charles for what they were promised, plus some."

"So the former employees could all be suspects. If the lawsuit wasn't going well, one or more of them might have decided to confront him on their own."

"Exactly. Mason gave me a list of the workers when I inquired about former employees. Of the five men laid off, I've established reliable alibis for all but two: the farm manager, Bill Parker, and a recent hire, Glen Collins."

"So two more suspects." I groaned.

"Looks like it, which brings the total back up to ten."

"Eleven," I added as I read the letter in my hand. "It looks like Charles was being sued by someone other than his ex-employees."

"Really? Who?"

"Some guy by the name of Raymond Wells. He owns a restaurant named Ray's and claims he ordered a dozen heritage turkeys for a high-class fund-raiser that was held at his establishment two months ago, but instead of receiving heritage turkeys he was delivered regular ones. He claims that the mix-up completely ruined his event and cost him tens of thousands of dollars in potential business. He was suing Charles for fifty thousand dollars."

I knew that heritage turkeys were considered to be the Rolls-Royces of turkeys, and upscale customers paid a pretty penny for them. If I'd paid upward of a hundred dollars a bird and was delivered a common, twenty-dollar one, I'd be pretty mad, too.

"Who serves turkey at a high-class fund-raiser in September?" Zak asked.

I shrugged. "It doesn't seem like an obvious choice unless they planned to prepare them in some special way. Still, would the guy have been mad enough to kill Charles over them?"

"Wells must know that if he killed Charles he'd never get his money. It sort of makes him an unlikely suspect."

"Unless he lost the suit and was out for revenge. I say we should add him to the list and check him out."

"Agreed." Zak added his name to the list he kept on his laptop. "The others should be back any minute. We should button this up and pick up where we left off tomorrow."

I started arranging the desk to resemble the way we had found it. "Ellie is making fettuccini for dinner. Do you want to join us?"

"Yeah. I'll drop you off, head home, shower and change, and then come back over. I'll bring the wine."

"I have wine."

"Yeah, but mine doesn't come in a box."

"My wine isn't in a box," I defended.

Zak just smiled.

"It's not," I insisted.

"Tree cutting three years ago," Zak reminded me, "I came home for the holiday and Levi invited me to meet you guys up at Tolleys' Peak. When I got there, you were all drinking wine out of paper cups. When I made a comment about that, you pointed out that the wine had originated in a box, so what difference did it make?"

"That was different. We were on a *picnic*," I emphasized. "You do understand the concept of a picnic?"

"I do. I'm just giving you a bad time. I can't remember the last time I had as much fun as I did that day on the mountain. I'm really looking forward to boxed wine and chili dogs again this year. I haven't even had a tree the past couple of years."

"Why not?"

Zak shrugged. "I was overseas and there wasn't anyone to share the holiday with, so I didn't bother."

"But you love Christmas." When we were growing up, Zak was known for his ridiculous antics during the holiday season. "You were always the one to plan holiday outings and give everyone outlandish presents."

"Do you still have those sweatshirts I bought you when we were in high school?" Zak laughed.

"Heck no," I lied. I actually did have them, but I'd never admit it after the fuss I put up when Zak insisted on giving them to me. I will admit to being diminutive in size, but I found it cruel that Zak bought me clothing that obviously originated in the children's department while he gifted both Levi and Ellie with presents they could actually use.

"Too bad. I especially liked the one with the reindeer."

I threw the pen that was sitting on the desk at Zak's chest. "Buying those stupid sweatshirts was mean and you know it."

"I know," Zak admitted. "I really am sorry, but you'd get so mad. It was adorable."

I turned off the desk lamp and picked up the backpack I'd left on the floor next to my feet. The last thing I wanted to do was awaken the complicated emotions I carried as a result of my tumultuous relationship with the boy Zak had once been. "I guess we should head out. Chances are the heirs will be back soon."

"I'm ready if you are. I've been thinking about Ellie's homemade sauce ever since you mentioned it."

Chapter 6

By the time Zak and I returned to the boathouse, Levi had arrived and was helping Ellie with dinner. Zak dropped me off and then headed home to shower and change. I couldn't help but overhear bits of the conversation my two best friends were having as I combed my hair and dressed in comfortable jeans and a sweater. I was unable to make out every word that was said, but I picked up on enough to get the gist of it.

As I mentioned before, Levi has recently hooked up with a yoga instructor who moved to town and opened a studio a few months ago. Being a fitness buff himself, his choice of romantic partner makes total sense. Levi has always tended to play the field, and his conquests have changed more often than the seasons, but based on the way he was going on and on about his new squeeze, I guessed this particular relationship had matured beyond the casual dating phase.

I felt bad for Ellie. Based on the way Levi was gushing over Barbie, I was convinced he didn't have a clue that Ellie had developed feelings of a romantic kind for him. At first I suspected Levi *had* picked up on Ellie's subtle signals, prompting him to enter into his rapidly evolving relationship with Barbie as a way to diffuse the potentially complicated situation, but Levi wasn't cruel. If he was aware of Ellie's feelings, he wouldn't be going on and on the way he was.

I tied back my hair in a scarf and made my way down from my loft bedroom to the kitchen. "Something smells wonderful," I complimented.

"I made stuffed mushrooms as an appetizer while we wait," Ellie informed me.

"They smell great."

"They need a few more minutes in the oven. How was your first day on the farm?"

"Interesting." I sat down on one of the bar stools that lined the counter separating the kitchen from the main living space. Levi poured me a glass of wine and slid it across to me. "We managed to whittle down the suspect list from fourteen to eight, but then we discovered three new suspects, so now we're back up to eleven."

"Anyone care to fill me in?" Levi asked.

I was tired and really didn't want to rehash the whole thing yet again, but I could tell Levi was curious, and if it had been me in the dark, I'd want to be filled in on all the juicy details.

"I found out that Charles Tisdale, the man who owned the turkey farm where Jeremy and I have been temporarily employed, was murdered. It looks like he was hit over the head with a blunt object the night before Jeremy was contacted about the job. I'm not a hundred percent certain, but it appears that no one, with the possible exception of the attorney, realizes the man was murdered."

"So why are *you* investigating?" Levi asked.

"I needed a distraction," I explained. "Besides, I never can resist a good mystery."

"I guess that's true," Levi acknowledged.

"So who are the suspects?"

I filled him in on the whole complicated affair, listing all the players in the most logical order I could come up with.

"You realize this sounds like a cheesy movie?" Levi laughed. "Guy dies and leaves four children by three women, as well as a mistress and a love child."

"Holly is Dolly's daughter and unrelated to Charles, so therefore not a love child," I corrected, "but otherwise you're spot-on. It does seem like the plot for a cheesy movie."

"Okay, so who was eliminated and who remains?" Levi asked.

"Zak eliminated Holly, who arrived after the death. Leroy never married, so we eliminated his wife. We also eliminated Peggy's husband and Brent's mother, both of whom are dead. Lola lives in Los Angeles and Penelope in Florida."

"How are you keeping all of this straight?" Levi wondered.

"I wrote everything down." I showed him my notebook. I passed it across the counter for his consideration. There were a lot of suspects, which made the task of investigating each for motive and alibi complicated, so I'd decided to group them into those who were heirs, those who were on the property but were not heirs, and those who were related in some way but were neither heirs nor present at the time of Charles's death.

"Do these people know you're investigating them?" Levi wondered.

"No. Zak is pretending to be a prospective buyer for the farm. So far no one seems to suspect that there's anything more than that going on. In fact I don't think anyone is paying much attention to any of us. The group that has assembled seems preoccupied with their own parts in the drama. Zak and Jeremy have both been wandering around talking to people and no one has said a word about it."

"Speaking of Zak, he just pulled up, and the mushrooms are done." Ellie removed a tray of sizzling appetizers from the oven.

"Those look fantastic." Levi tried to pick one up off the cookie sheet, but Ellie slapped his hand.

"You're going to burn yourself. Wait until I can put them on a serving plate."

"Did you think to bring horseradish?" Levi asked.

"I did."

"A woman after my own heart." Levi grinned, and Ellie smiled shyly.

It's really odd for me to see Ellie acting so tentative around Levi. Like I said before, the three of us have been best friends since kindergarten. Ellie has always treated Levi like a brother. As strange as it is for me to watch her awkwardness around the boy she used to throw snowballs at, it must be *really* strange for her.

"Let me help you with that." Levi took the hot tray from Ellie. "You've been slaving away since I've been here. Pour yourself a glass of wine and relax."

Ellie actually blushed as Levi took her by the shoulders, turned her around, and gave her a friendly swat on the butt as he pointed her toward the living area.

"As long as you're both here," Levi began as he slid the mushrooms onto a serving platter, "I've been meaning to ask you about Thanksgiving. I thought I'd ask Barbie to join us, if you don't mind."

Ellie's smile faded and I was saved having to reply as Zak walked through the front door bearing wine I was sure would cost more than my weekly grocery budget. Every year my dad, grandfather, and me, Ellie and her mom, and Levi, who has no family in town, get together to prepare a giant feast. In all of the years we've been doing it, none of us has ever brought a date, even though many of the times one or more of us has been involved in a relationship of one type or another. Thanksgiving has always been family time, so Levi asking to bring a date was huge. I had planned to ask the gang about including Zak this year, but I think his inclusion would have met with approval across the board, while Barbie's attendance promised nothing but controversy.

"That's fine," Ellie managed a plastic smile as she answered Levi. "And Zak, you're invited as well."

"Invited where?" Zak asked, because he hadn't been privy to the first part of the conversation.

"Thanksgiving. This year it's Zoe's turn to host, so we'll all meet here."

Zak looked at me before answering.

"I'd planned to ask you. You can bring the wine," I joked, as I accepted the bottles he'd brought with him. Sure enough, I was certain one of them retailed for over a hundred dollars.

"I'd love to come," Zak said.

"I may bring someone as well," Ellie added. "Do you think there'll be room?"

I did a mental calculation. My dad and Pappy, Levi and Barbie, Ellie, her mother, and her mystery date, Zak and me, and the small pack of dogs we owned among us. It was going to be tight.

"How about we have the dinner at my place?" Zak offered. "I've wanted to have everyone over for a housewarming of sorts."

Zak is in the process of buying my maternal grandfather's estate, a huge residence that hugs the shoreline just around the bend from my little boathouse. Zak had mentioned that my grandfather didn't want to bother with moving the furniture, so they'd made everything right down to the linens part of the deal. I knew the dining room table would seat at least twenty-five, and with twenty-thousand square feet of living space, tripping over each other wouldn't be a problem.

"You don't mind?" I asked.

"Not at all. I'd love to host the event. I have plenty of room to stretch out, and tons of room for the dogs to run around and play without being underfoot."

"I'll come by early and help you with the cooking," I offered.

"I'll have coffee and sticky buns," Zak promised.

"Awesome." Levi clapped. "It looks like we have a plan. I wanted to bring Barbie to the community dinner, but she wasn't into it. A feast in Zak's mansion is definitely more up her alley."

"Speaking of the community dinner," I decided to change the subject, "I heard the committee voted to change it from the Wednesday to the Tuesday before Thanksgiving."

Ellie, Levi, and I are members of the Ashton Falls Events Committee, a community group formed to oversee the planning and implementation of the myriad celebrations and events designed to bring the almighty tourist dollar from the large cities below, up the mountain to our tiny alpine town. Each month there's a major fund-raising effort, without which the volunteer fire department, free public library, afterschool sports and activities programs, and subsidized day care, wouldn't be possible. Up until two weeks ago, when the county fired me and decided to close the animal control and rehabilitation facility, a good portion of my own job funding had come from fund-raising as well. With the closure of the facility, I was unsure whether I'd remain on the committee, and I'd missed the last two meetings.

"I thought I'd mentioned it," Ellie confirmed. "The group is hoping there'll be less of a conflict with everyone's travel plans. You know," Ellie looked directly at me, "you really should try to make the next meeting. I realize you no longer need the funding the group provides, but the group could still use your help."

I winced. Ellie was right. I seriously needed to get over myself and join the living. I knew the committee was depending on me to organize the Christmas event the following month, but I'd been so self-involved that I'd let everyone down. I certainly wasn't the first person to be fired from a dream job and I certainly wouldn't be the last. I was tied up with my duty at the turkey farm the following week but promised to help out with the dinner and attend the meeting the week after that.

Chapter 7

Since the following day was Sunday and Donovan's, the store my dad owns and operates, was closed, he volunteered to come over to stay with Maggie. I'd like to go on record as stating that my dad is great. I mean really, really great. Not only did he raise me on his own but he has been there for me every day, loving me, supporting me, and adopting the various hard-to-place animals I end up bringing to his doorstep when no one else seems quite right.

As arranged, he showed up at seven o'clock with his dogs, Tucker and Kiva, in tow.

"So how's our little mom-to-be?" Dad asked.

"She's doing well. I can feel the pups moving around, so I figure it won't be long. I have a birthing box set up for her in my bedroom should the blessed event take place while I'm away, and of course you have Scott's number."

"It was nice that you suggested breakfast," Dad commented. "It's been a while since we had a chance to catch up."

"It has," I agreed as I set a platter with scrambled eggs and toast on the oak dining table. "So what's new in your life?"

I prayed he'd bring up the subject of my mother so I wouldn't have to confront him with what I was beginning to consider a major betrayal. Zak had let it slip a few weeks ago that my mother was not only in town but had been for several months and hadn't bothered to contact me in all that time. To make matters worse, I found out that my dad actually had had dinner with the woman and likewise failed to mention it, even though I see him on an almost daily basis. I've been waiting for him to broach the subject but have finally decided if he doesn't do it this morning, I'm going to bring it up myself.

"Not much," Dad replied to my question.

"How was your date?"

"Date?"

"The week before Halloween, when I came in to Donovan's to talk to you about Kiva, we were trying to work out a time to have dinner and you mentioned you had a date on that Monday. I was just wondering how it went. You ended up canceling dinner with me on Tuesday, and we haven't really had a chance to talk since."

I noticed that my dad was going out of his way to avoid eye contact. Not a good sign in my book. I've gone over the situation again and again in my head but have been unable to make sense of any of it. My dad and I are close, and as far as I know, we never keep secrets from each other. The fact that he'd been in contact with my mother and hadn't bothered to mention it to me felt like a betrayal of trust.

For the record, for those of you who don't really know me, I tend to be just a tad OCD when it comes to my most important relationships. While I can go with the flow in many areas of my life, I have a compulsive need to maintain a state of equilibrium in my close relationships. I know this about myself, and in spite of my amateur psychoanalysis of my emotional foible, I've been unable to change the insane behavior that follows an imbalance in this desired state.

My dad seemed uncomfortable with my line of questioning, and I knew the kind thing to do was let him off the hook; after all, he was here in my home at seven o'clock in the morning to do me a huge favor.

"I know about Mom," I blurted out. "How could you know she was in town and not tell me?"

Dad took my hand from across the table. "I know I should have told you. I'm sorry."

"Sorry?" I screeched. See: crazy. "You had dinner with my mother and you're *sorry* you forgot to mention it?"

"I didn't forget," Dad admitted. "It was a complicated situation and I didn't want to upset you needlessly. I admit I handled it badly."

"Complicated?" My eyes began to tear up. "How could things be any more complicated than they have my entire life?"

"I'll tell you what you want to know if you can rein in the drama-queen routine and listen to what I have to say with an open mind."

Did I mention that my dad knows me well enough to realize when I'm being ridiculously dramatic, which I have to confess is more often than I'd like?

"Okay." I took a deep breath and dried my eyes. "No more hysterics. I promise."

My dad fidgeted with his napkin while I pulled myself together. "Your mom came to see me several months ago," he began. "She was engaged to a prince from some small country I've never heard of. As she neared the day of her nuptials, she began to regret some of the choices she'd made in her life. She said that she had lived the life she always thought she wanted: world travel, exotic love affairs, thrilling adventures. Yet, somehow, she felt empty. She began to think about us and realized that maybe what she really wanted was the one thing she'd had all along but had thrown away. She asked me if I could forgive her, if I could make room for her in my life."

Tears started to trail down my cheeks again, but this time they weren't tears from Zoe the crazy but Zoe the abandoned child. "She didn't want to see me?" I whispered.

"She did." My dad squeezed my hand. "But your mom has hurt you so much already. She's broken more promises to you than she's ever kept. I didn't want you to get hurt. I didn't want either of us to get hurt again."

I knew my dad had loved my mother his whole life. She'd used him and then tossed him aside. But he'd never stopped loving her, which probably explains why he's never really dated.

"So you had dinner with her?" I prompted.

"I agreed to see her on a limited basis if she agreed to stay away from you until we decided what, if anything, this might mean for us. I love your mother. I always have and I always will. I guess there has always been a part of me waiting for her. When she showed up on my doorstep and offered me my heart's desire, I wasn't sure how to react."

For once in my life I kept my mouth shut and listened to what my father was trying to tell me.

"At first I was reluctant to let her back into my life even a tiny bit, but then she rented a cottage on the beach and I could see she was serious about staying. After a month or so, I agreed to a dinner, and she told me that she wanted to have another chance with me if I'd let her."

My heart sank. I knew my mother had left town more than two weeks ago, so obviously things hadn't worked out.

"We went out a few more times and it was," Dad paused, "perfect. We laughed and we cried. It felt like the woman I'd always loved was back in my life. I was going to tell you. I thought we could finally be a family. But . . ."

"Then she left," I finished.

"I guess things got too intense for her," my dad said sadly. "In many ways you're a lot like your mother. You tend to go a little insane if your most important relationships are disturbed in any way and your mom tends to go a little insane if the people she cares most about get too close. She's as afraid of letting people in as you are of letting them go."

I noticed moisture in my dad's eyes that broke my heart. "Did she go back to her prince?"

My dad shrugged. "I don't know. I guess. She doesn't really love him, so she'll probably be able to marry him."

I know it sounds insane, but I totally understood where my mom was coming from. The thing we both feared was strong and uncontrolled emotion. We wanted our relationships to be neat and tidy, without any of the messy by-products that come from change or emotional risk. I know that's why I've had such a hard time letting Zak in, and why Ellie's feelings for Levi scare me to death. There's a part of me that wants, even needs, to keep things steady and stable.

"I'm sorry." I got up, walked around the table, and hugged my dad. We both cried for the woman we loved who could never love us back.

Chapter 8

"Something wrong?" Jeremy asked as I stood staring at the pens of turkeys.

"Doesn't it seem like there are fewer birds now than there were yesterday?"

"I don't know." Jeremy frowned. "Maybe. Did you think to count them as we checked them over?"

"No; you?"

"No. It didn't really occur to me to do it. I mean, where are they going to go?"

Jeremy had a point. Still, something felt off.

"Maybe we should count them today," I suggested. "You mentioned they were inventoried when they were placed in the pens. We can compare the numbers."

"Okay," Jeremy agreed.

"Have you seen Zak?" I wondered.

"He was talking to Margaret the last time I saw him. He mentioned something about taking a walk."

I knew Zak was most likely just pumping Margaret for information, but I couldn't completely suppress jealous Zoe from rearing her ugly head. Honestly, most of the time I feel like I'm a complete victim to my irrational emotions. In this instance, however, I made a decision to count turkeys with Jeremy and assume Zak was doing exactly what I'd asked him to do and not off flirting with Peggy's very single daughter.

"We're short thirty birds," Jeremy confirmed several hours later.

"Coyotes?" I ventured a guess.

"Possible, but I doubt it. I was never more than hearing distance away and I never heard a ruckus. Besides, if a coyote had attacked, there would be evidence."

By evidence I knew he meant blood, guts, and feathers.

"Poachers?" I guessed again.

"Maybe. Birds were missing from each of the enclosures, which seems to point to the fact that someone took them but hoped it wouldn't be noticed. If coyotes were the culprit, they most likely would have attacked a single enclosure."

"Should we tell someone?"

Jeremy thought about it. "I wouldn't. Let's just keep an eye on things to see if any more birds turn up missing. It looks like Zak is coming back. Why don't you see what he found out and I'll finish up here."

Zak had returned from his three-hour walk with Margaret just in time for her to change for the funeral. I knew the family would be gone several hours at least, and this might very well be the last time everyone would be gone all at once. I helped Jeremy for a while longer and then followed Zak into the house. As I had the day before, I took off my shoes, but this time I had coveralls to remove as well, to minimize the risk of tracking turkey dung across the spotlessly clean floor.

"So?" I asked as we set up in the office. "Did you find out anything relevant from Margaret?"

"I did," Zak confirmed. "Margaret and her mother arrived Thursday afternoon, shortly after Leroy, who, according to Margaret, arrived at three o'clock in the afternoon on the day Pike found the body. They drove, so this is a little hard to verify."

"That doesn't mean they didn't kill Charles," I pointed out. "They could have come to the farm, offed him, and then left, only to return after the others did."

"That's true," Zak acknowledged. "If the estate is divided equally, Peggy stands to inherit ten million of the fifty million dollars Charles has been sitting on, plus a fifth of the estate he built on his own."

"Wait." Something had occurred to me. "Jeremy said Charles disinherited Peggy when she married a man he didn't approve of. Wouldn't that mean she would receive nothing?"

"My thought exactly," Zak said. "According to Margaret, Charles disinherited Peggy in his heart, but he never did from his will. His estate was always to be divided between his four children. He recently added Holly, dividing the assets into five equal shares. When Bertram went to jail for killing his wife, Charles altered the will so that his share would go to Brent."

"Did Margaret find it odd that you were asking all these questions?"

"Not really. I was careful to work the questions casually into our conversation and she seemed happy to have someone to talk to. I got the impression that she is a very lonely woman who doesn't get a lot of male attention."

"So she was just flattered that you asked to take a walk with her and didn't stop to question why."

"Pretty much."

"Okay, so according to Margaret, Leroy arrived Thursday afternoon. Can we verify that?"

"I'm checking into it."

"Okay, so who *can* we eliminate?"

"Raymond Wells, the man who filed the lawsuit, apparently settled out of court. I spoke briefly to Mason, who confirmed that he was quite happy with the settlement he received."

"Mason told you that?"

"He did. As a prospective buyer of the property, it is my right to know about any potential lawsuits that could result in a lien against the property."

"That makes sense. So where does that leave us?"

"Oliver and Olivia, Peggy and Margaret, Leroy, Brent, Mason, and the farm workers, Bill Parker and Glen Collins."

"Is that it?"

"The mistress, Dolly Robinson, hasn't been seen by anyone including Holly since the murder. Holly confirmed that she's been staying at her place, but her mother hasn't come home."

"I thought Holly learned of Charles's death from her mother."

"She did. Dolly called Holly and informed her of Charles's death and her inclusion in the will, but when Holly got here, Dolly was nowhere to be found. Holly figured her mom just needed some time to herself, but when she didn't show up for the viewing yesterday, she began to get worried."

"So who do you think did it?" I asked Zak.

"Honestly, I have no idea."

"So what now? We have an hour and a half at least until the troops return. How should we use that time?"

Zak grinned.

"Pervert," I teased.

"Why don't you search Peggy, Margaret, Leroy, and Brent's rooms, and I'll look around in here some more and then check out Oliver and Olivia's room? Let's plan to be out of the house in an hour. I wouldn't want to get caught by someone returning early."

I felt like a cat burglar as I made my way upstairs. I really wanted to figure out who killed Charles Tisdale, but I have to admit I felt strange going through everyone's personal possessions. A search of Peggy's room revealed that she had a cosmetic collection that would rival Estée Lauder's, but other than confirming what I already expected about her overly loud and gaudy wardrobe, I didn't come up with anything really interesting about her participation in Charles's death.

Margaret's room was neat and organized and featured a stack of romance novels on the bedside table as well as a scented candle and a framed photo of her with a young man wearing a military uniform. I couldn't help but wonder about the fate of the young man in the photo. Based on Margaret's interest in Zak, I was willing to bet he was no longer in the picture.

Leroy's room revealed a wardrobe selection equally gaudy to Peggy's, as well as a thick legal document declaring Leroy's intent to sue Charles for unpaid back wages if he didn't negotiate a settlement to address the issue. I remembered that Leroy had worked on the farm for a good part of his life under the false assumption that he would one day inherit the property from his father. If the threat of a lawsuit hadn't produced the desired result, could Leroy have decided to take matters into his own hands?

I took a photo of the top page of the document with my phone and made my way to Brent's room at the end of the hall. Like Margaret's, Brent's was neat and tidy. His clothes were hung strategically by color, his bedside table free of clutter other than the thriller he was reading, and his private bath was spotless, with his toiletries lined neatly on the counter. I was about to leave the room when I noticed the drawer of the bedside table half open. I looked inside and found an old journal, worn and yellow with age. I turned to the first page and gasped. It seemed I'd found my killer.

Chapter 9

Zak had to meet with his attorney regarding the purchase of my grandfather's property, so I was on my own as I drove to the turkey farm the following morning. I found that I really missed his company, which in some ways was bizarre, considering it was only a few weeks since I had been avoiding his presence at any cost. My dad had to work today, as did Levi and Ellie, so I had dropped off Charlie and Maggie at Donovan's. Zak was going to pick them up when he finished his business meeting and then stay with them until I got home. I'm not sure why exactly, but I had the feeling that today was the day Maggie's hopefully healthy bundles of joy would be making their way into the world.

Jeremy and I were busy with the turkeys well into the afternoon. The day progressed quickly as I filled him in on the progress of the murder investigation. Not only had our search uncovered Leroy's legal action against his father but the fact that Brent had a very revealing journal written by Charles as a young man, catapulted him to the top of our suspect list. A cursory read the previous day had revealed that Charles began writing the journal as a young man seeking freedom from the tyranny of an abusive and overbearing father. The journal detailed his journey from subjugation and poverty to riches and independence through hard work and untold sacrifice. The journal ended with his confession that he *had* been giving belladonna to Amelia and although it was an accident, he most likely *was* the catalyst for her untimely death. I wasn't sure where Brent had gotten the journal or if the contents were the subject of their recent encounter, but my gut told me I should move seemingly mild-mannered Brent to the top of our suspect list.

As we had the previous day, we counted the birds as we inspected and then moved them. If thirty missing turkeys presented a mystery the day before, the fact that we had extra turkeys today was outright bizarre.

"I don't get it." Jeremy scratched his head. "Yesterday we were short thirty and today we have three over the original inventory."

"Do you think we miscounted?" I wondered.

"We must have. I thought we were being careful, but for the life of me I can't come up with any other explanation for the discrepancy in number."

"Maybe someone took them and then returned them?"

"Why would anyone do that?"

I had no idea.

"Besides," Jeremy added, "if someone *did* borrow them, why would we have three more than we began with now?"

"Interest?" I speculated.

Jeremy rolled his eyes at my ridiculous suggestion.

"I guess we'll just have to be a little more careful tomorrow," I said. "We'll figure out a way to double-check our numbers and see where we stand."

"Good idea."

"So is the family still assembled?" I asked.

"So far no one has left. I guess there's going to be an informal gathering among the various attorneys to identify any and all challenges to the will as it stands. Last I heard, the meet and complain is scheduled for

Thursday. I'd be willing to bet no one leaves before then."

Today was Monday, which gave me a few more days to snoop around.

"Has the vet come by to look at the sick birds?" I wondered. The previous day we'd identified eight birds exhibiting symptoms that most closely resembled intoxication. They stumbled around, lacking direction and coordination. I know it's crazy to even contemplate, but if I didn't know better, I'd swear that somehow they'd gotten into the abandoned still I'd found at the edge of the property. Pike had mentioned that the still had belonged to the previous owner of the property and hadn't been operational for years, but based on the behavior of the birds we'd isolated, I wondered if Charles hadn't resurrected the dinosaur without anyone knowing about it.

"He thinks they may have ingested something poisonous. He's having the feed tested and said we should be extra diligent about watching for similar behavior in other birds."

"He thinks someone could have poisoned the feed?"

"Not necessarily, but he wanted to eliminate the possibility. The reality is that if the feed is contaminated, all the birds would be sick. But only eight seem to be infected, so he's considering other options. He took one of the birds with him and said he'd call me when he found something out."

"Who knew turkeys could be so much trouble?" I lamented. "I noticed Holly arrived on the property a little while ago. If you don't need me, I thought I'd try to have a chat with her. I'd like to get a better feel for her mom's relationship with Charles."

"Go ahead. We're almost done here."

Holly appeared to be about Brent's age. She had long black hair, dark eyes, and olive skin. In spite of her age, her style of dress and immaculate grooming made her appear both mature and sophisticated. I found her sitting in a lounge chair near one of the waterfalls, bundled up in tan slacks and a warm cashmere sweater.

"Mind if I join you?" I sat down across from her without waiting for an answer. "It's a beautiful day for this time of year."

"It is," she agreed. "I was getting tired of sitting alone at my mother's and remembered how lovely the garden is."

"So your mother hasn't returned?"

Holly frowned at me before answering. I imagine she was trying to decide how much I knew and how much she should reveal. "No. I spoke to Oliver about it, and he said he'd look into it, but as far as I can tell, no one seems to be looking into anything other than who should get what."

"Were you surprised to be included in Charles's will?"

Holly shrugged, her long straight hair draped over one shoulder. If I had to guess, I'd say she was of Hawaiian descent. She had a look of tropical elegance about her. "Not really," she answered. "Charles is," she hesitated, "*was* a bitter and lonely old man with strong opinions that ruled his life and isolated him from the people he should have loved. By the time I met him, he was locked inside an emotional prison from which I think even he realized he'd never be able to escape. I've always been the type of person to pick up strays, whether human or animal. When I first met him, I could see his pain, so I spent most of my vacation with my mother being the biggest pain in the ass I could possibly be."

I laughed. "What do you mean by that?"

"I would sit and talk to Charles for hours on end. He absolutely hated it. He ranted and raved and demanded I leave, but the more he pushed me away, the more determined I was to break though the shell he'd built. It broke my heart that he had no one."

"He had your mom," I pointed out.

Holly laughed. "Hardly. My mom is great. She raised me on her own, sent me to culinary school, and is helping me start my own bistro. She lived her life with no other goal than to give me everything I ever wanted. Unfortunately, the way my mother chose to fund my life was to hook up with old men with more money than sense. She never stole from them. Everything she received was freely given, but I can assure you that she never loved or even cared for any of them. They were a means to an end, and in most cases they knew that and were fine with it."

"Your mother must be a beautiful woman," I speculated. I figured she'd have to be to win the affections of so many rich men.

"She is. I love her very much, but I have to admit I don't really understand her."

"So I'm guessing you eventually got through to the old man?" I asked.

Holly smiled, a genuine, heartfelt smile that conveyed her true affection for the man her mother had bled for money. "I did. It took a while, but at some point he began to respond to my incessant chattering. He started to reveal parts of himself to me:

unmet hopes and dreams, regrets and broken promises."

If there was one thing our investigation had accomplished, it was the discovery that Charles Tisdale had been a monster who killed his wife and then refused to help his children in their times of greatest need, even though he had more than enough means to do so. I found Holly's genuine affection for the man confusing.

"Do you think your mother's disappearance is in some way connected to Charles's death?" I asked.

Holly looked startled. "You think something happened to her?"

"Don't you?"

"Not really. I hate to admit it, but I think she's moved on."

"Moved on? Charles passed away on Wednesday. Your mother was gone by the time you got here on Thursday. Surely she wouldn't . . ."

Holly smiled sadly. "She would. Her relationships are and have always been a means to an end. The money dries up and she's gone."

"But she loves you," I pointed out. "Surely she'd stay around to see you. She knew you'd be here."

"Yeah, I guess that's why I'm worried. Still, if I find out she hooked up with some guy and took off for the Bahamas, I won't be surprised. Keep in mind that Charles was more than forty years older than my mother. In her mind he was her benefactor, nothing more."

I felt sorry for Holly. My mom was a flake, but I had my dad, and he was fantastic. Holly didn't appear to have anyone.

"How are the others treating you?" I asked. "They didn't seem thrilled you were getting a fifth of the estate."

"Oliver and Olivia have officially challenged the will. Leroy doesn't seem to care, as long as he gets his cut, and Peggy and Margaret just want to wrap this whole thing up as quickly as possible. I think they resent the fact that I was included, but they don't want the estate tied up in court, so they're willing to let me have my cut if they can get their share that much faster."

"And Brent?"

Holly frowned. "I'm not sure. Brent was really nice at first. Even flirty. But he's been sort of withdrawn ever since the funeral. I get the feeling something is up, but I have no idea what."

"Did your mother have a relationship with anyone in the family other than Charles?"

"Why do you ask?" Holly seemed suspicious of my questions, and I guess I couldn't blame her. I was after all the hired help and really had no reason to be asking so many personal questions.

"It just occurred to me that maybe one of the other family members had spoken to your mother since Charles's death and might have an idea of where she'd gone," I offered.

"My mom wasn't really accepted by the group, so it wasn't like there were any big family dinners, if that's what you're talking about," Holly shared. "But my mom did have an acquaintance of sorts with Olivia."

"Olivia? She seems so . . ."

"Cold? Yeah, she is. The only reason I even knew the two had met was because my mom mentioned that

Olivia sought her out in the hope that she could assist her in her quest to convince Charles to help them out financially. My mom didn't have a lot of influence over Charles, but she had some, and it sounded like Olivia was desperate."

"I guess that makes sense. Have you asked Olivia about your mother's whereabouts?"

"Yeah. She said she didn't know and in fact hadn't spoken to her in quite some time. I'm not really surprised by that. I doubt my mom would have helped Olivia even if she'd been able to. If my mom thought she could get extra money out of Charles, she would have kept it for herself."

Holly's phone rang while I sat trying to wrap my head around everything she'd said. She looked at the caller ID, then excused herself.

Olivia and Dolly had at a minimum met. I wasn't sure this was important, but I filed it away for future reference. Given the fact that Oliver and Olivia were challenging the will, thereby delaying everyone's departure, I was willing to bet they hadn't killed Charles. It made sense that if they had, they would have been more than anxious to leave. Peggy and Margaret, on the other hand, were displaying behavior more akin to a guilty party. I still hadn't decided what, if any, relevance Brent's possession of Charles's journal had to do with his death and I wasn't sure what to make of Dolly's disappearance. Zak would be at the house when I returned. Maybe I'd run everything past him and see what he thought.

Chapter 10

Scott called while I was at the farm and told me that he had a nutritional supplement he wanted me to start giving Maggie after the puppies were born. He'd been by the boathouse earlier to check on her and agreed that the pups would most likely be born in the next twelve hours. He hadn't had the supplement with him at the time but wondered if I could stop by and pick it up on my way through town.

It was dark by the time I pulled into Ashton Falls. The town where I was born and raised holds a special place in my heart. Known as the event capital of the Timberland Mountains, Ashton Falls is a quaint village nestled on the shore of a large deepwater lake, surrounded by hundreds of miles of thick evergreen forest. The town was originally developed by Ashton Montgomery, a multimillionaire and my great-grandfather on my mother's side. At one time all the land in the mountain basin where Ashton Falls now resides was owned by the Montgomerys, but, unlike Ashton, his three sons weren't thrilled with the mountain way of life and had moved from the area as soon as they were old enough.

After Ashton died, his sons had divided the land and begun selling it off, keeping in the family only a few prime pieces of property, including the isolated bay where my converted boathouse sits. Of the three sons, my grandfather Preston is the only one who continued to visit Ashton Falls after their father's death. Every summer he'd bring his wife, three sons, and daughter, my mother, to the mansion he built overlooking the lake for two months of what he laughably labeled rugged mountain living. That, by the way, is how my mother met my father and yours truly was conceived.

The veterinary hospital, where I was to meet Scott, was just north of the animal shelter where I used to work. Scott had volunteered many hours at the shelter, and during the time we'd worked together we'd become good friends. As I passed the shelter, I gasped. The day after the county closed the place, they'd stuck a for-sale sign on it, although there had still been a part of me that hoped the county would realize the error of their ways and ask Jeremy and me to return to work. As I stopped in front of the old building and stared at the SOLD sign, I knew in my heart that the thing I most longed for in the world was good and officially gone.

In many ways I felt like I was trapped in a bad dream in which I was left alone and adrift in the middle of an endless sea. I'd worked for the county shelter since I was old enough to serve as a volunteer. I'd spent summers during high school, as well as every afternoon during the school year, caring for the animals that felt like family. After high school I had taken the necessary classes and applied for a full-time position. When word came through that I'd landed the job, I'd really felt that my career was set for life. I'd worked my way into the position of facility manager and hoped to use my influence to change the county's antiquated policies regarding mandatory termination after a specified number of days.

I guess the good I might have done will go unknown. To this day, I'm not sure whether I'd have done things differently if I'd had the chance to do them again. A killer was caught, and that was important, but the dogs and cats that might have lived and now will most likely die seem much too great a price to pay.

I continued on to the veterinary hospital, where I greeted Scott.

"I'm glad you were able to stop by." Scott hugged me. "Maggie is doing a lot better. I can see that you've been taking really good care of her."

"I've done everything I know to do," I confirmed. "She's such a sweetie. I hope that delivering her pups isn't going to be too much for her."

"She seems to have regained her strength, and the pups seem healthy. You never know what might go wrong, but I'm betting she'll do okay. We'll want her to nurse if she can after the pups are born, so it's important you start her on the supplement right away."

"I will. I noticed a sold sign on the shelter. Any idea who bought it?"

"I'm not sure. I overheard some clients talking about a rich developer, but that might have been nothing more than small-town gossip."

"A developer? You think someone might tear it down?"

"It seems likely. I'm not sure what good the building is to anyone other than an animal shelter."

"Yeah, I guess." I couldn't believe how sad the thought made me. I mean, I get it. There aren't a lot of businesses that can make use of hallways full of cages, but I'd spent a lot of time in that building. It was going to kill me to see it destroyed.

When I arrived at the boathouse, Zak was in the kitchen, cooking something that smelled like heaven. Charlie trotted over to the door and greeted me with unbridled joy, but Maggie was nowhere to be found. I greeted Charlie, who wasn't about to let me pass until I'd done so, and then wandered in to speak to Zak.

"Maggie?" I asked.

"Upstairs in your room. No puppies yet, but I have the feeling it won't be long. I'm making my macaroni and chicken casserole. I'll stick the garlic bread in the oven if you want to change."

"The casserole smells wonderful." I opened the oven door and peeked inside. "What's in it?"

"Family secret." Zak grinned.

"I want to check on Maggie and take a quick shower. Give me twenty minutes."

I scurried up the stairs to the loft that serves as my bedroom. Maggie, who was curled up in the corner of my closet, didn't get up but wagged her tail as I bent down to greet her. "I see you're not a fan of the birthing box I set up."

It appeared that Zak had moved my shoes to the side and made up a bed of blankets for the mom-to-be. I ran my hand over Maggie's distended stomach and felt for the pups as they moved into position. "It won't be long now," I promised the little dog. "I'm going to get cleaned up, and then I'll be back to check on you."

Maggie licked my hand as I rose to gather my clothes and make my way down to the bathroom. I turned the water on to heat as I stared out of the window to the dark forest beyond. When I'd first rescued Maggie, she was so thin that her bones protruded from her frail little frame. I figured there was no way her puppies would live, but Scott started her on a high-calorie, nutrient-dense diet and enough supplements to fill half a shelf in my kitchen cabinet.

I still worried about her ability to deliver without complications and the overall health of the puppies given their rough start, but I hoped that after two weeks of tender loving care, everything would go smoothly for the sweet little mother and her family.

After showering and changing into comfortable sweatpants and an oversize sweater, I checked on Maggie one more time before joining Zak in the kitchen. The cheesy pasta, crisp garden salad, and golden garlic bread was quite possibly the best meal I'd ever had. It didn't hurt that it was served with a glass of Zak's ridiculously expensive wine.

"So how goes the investigation?" Zak asked after we were seated.

"I don't have a lot of new information," I informed him. "Oliver and Olivia have contested the will, Peggy and Margaret want things wrapped up as quickly as possible, Leroy doesn't seem to care much one way or the other, Dolly is still missing, and Brent, who is in possession of Charles's deepest, most intimate thoughts, is acting withdrawn and secretive. Probably the most interesting thing I learned is that Holly seems to have genuinely cared about the old man. I had a brief discussion with her today and, of all the leeches at the estate, she seems to be the only one to truly give a damn about him, not just the money. How'd your meeting with your attorney go?"

"Good. The property should close by the end of the week."

"Congratulations." I held up my wineglass in a toast. "I wasn't sure about having a neighbor after all this time, but if I have to have one, I'm glad it's you."

Zak smiled.

"I noticed the old shelter has a sold sign on it," I commented. "I knew it would be sold eventually, but I have to be honest: a part of me really hoped the county would change its mind and reopen the facility. Ashton Falls really needs its own shelter. Running things from Bryton Lake may work out in the short-term, but having patrols drive the thirty miles up the mountain in the dead of winter is going to be a nightmare."

"I'm sure the county has taken that into account."

I frowned. It wasn't like Zak to so totally disregard my feelings. Here I was, pouring my heart out to him, and he was answering with logic.

"There's more bread in the kitchen," Zak offered.

"Thanks." I pushed away my plate. "I think I'll go and check on Maggie."

By the time I made my way upstairs, Maggie was deep in labor. I called to Zak as the first black-and-white puppy, a male, made its way into the world. Puppy number two was a black-and-tan female, followed by another black-and-white male.

"Do you think she's finished?" Zak asked.

It had been several hours and we all, including Maggie, were exhausted.

"It feels like she has one more," I answered.

Poor Maggie could barely hold her head up. I worried about her ability to deliver the last pup unassisted. "Maybe we should call Scott," I suggested.

"I'll call him. You stay with Maggie," Zak offered.

Zak called Scott, who was tied up with another house call but promised to be by as quickly as he could. I listened as he discussed Maggie's condition with Scott, while I softly encouraged my brave little mama to hang in just a little longer.

"Maybe we can help her out," Zak suggested.

"Hold her head and I'll see what I can do."

I gently helped work the last puppy, a tricolored female, from Maggie's body as Zak sat at her head and tried to keep her calm. The puppy was small—much smaller than the others—but she was alive and breathing. Tears streamed down my face as I offered a silent prayer of thanks.

Poor Maggie was exhausted, so Zak and I cleaned up the pups, then fed them with the formula and bottles Scott had given me.

"Do you think she's going to be okay?" I asked as Maggie slept with her head in my lap.

"I hope so." Zak sat on the floor next to me. "She had a rough time and lost a lot of blood, but she seems to be breathing okay, and the pain seems to be gone. We should stay with her until she wakes up."

Maggie started to whimper. I petted her gently as the puppies slept next to her.

"I'll get her some fresh water." Zak stood up.

It turned out to be a long night. Zak and I took turns sitting with Maggie, and we both pitched in to feed the puppies every few hours. But by the time the sun rose over the distant mountain, Maggie was awake and the danger had passed.

Chapter 11

Zak stayed at the boathouse with Maggie and her babies while I made my way to work. I considered calling Jeremy and telling him that I couldn't make it in, but the exhaustive routine we'd established really did require two bodies, and after downing a pot and a half of coffee, I felt awake enough to honor my commitment. When I pulled into the drive, I noticed that there was a sheriff's vehicle in front of the house. After parking in my usual spot behind the barn, I set off in search of Jeremy, who, I hoped, would be able to fill me in.

Jeremy was in the office pouring over inventory sheets when I found him. "What's going on?" I asked.

"The sheriff called a meeting of all of the heirs. I guess he finally decided it was time to tell them Charles was murdered. There are a couple of deputies here as well. They're going to interview everyone even remotely involved."

I realized that with the revelation of the murder the killer's hand might be forced, which could cause him or her to act. I needed to keep an eye on everyone remaining on our suspect list. I hoped the killer would panic and show his or her hand, with me conveniently around to notice.

"I'm afraid there's more," Jeremy added. "Holly's mother was found dead in the hills behind the farm. It looks like she's been there for several days."

"Oh my God. Poor Holly. Do they know what happened?"

"I overheard one of the deputies talking to Oliver. It appears that she, like Charles, was bludgeoned to death."

"What was she doing in the hills behind the farm?" I wondered.

"I have no idea. All I know is that her body was found early this morning by a man on horseback, and that it looked like it had been there for a while."

I knew Dolly had called Holly after Charles's death but that she wasn't at home when Holly arrived later that day and hadn't been seen since. My guess was that she'd been murdered sometime between her phone call to Holly and Holly's arrival in town. It wasn't likely Dolly had been on the property when Charles was killed; Pike had reported that Charles was alone in the house when he found him on the kitchen floor. I suppose someone must have called Dolly, who had called Holly. I had to wonder if Dolly was murdered in the spot where she was found or if she had been bludgeoned elsewhere and then moved to this remote location.

Dolly's murder added an interesting twist to the case. It seemed that several of the visitors had a reason to kill Charles, but whom among them also had a motive to kill her?

I was dying to know what the sheriff and his men had discovered, but I doubted it was going to do me any good to simply go and ask. I decided my best bet was to call Zak and see what, if anything, he was able to find out. In the meantime, Jeremy and I went about the task of feeding, counting, and rotating the turkeys.

"By the way," Jeremy informed me as we worked, "I talked to the vet this morning. The sick birds we discovered yesterday were suffering from milkweed poisoning."

I frowned. "I haven't noticed any milkweed on the property."

"That's because there isn't any. Milkweed is extremely toxic. Charles would have been careful to ensure that there wasn't any on the premises."

"The feed?" I guessed.

"The vet says no. The feed tested clean."

"So where did the birds come into contact with milkweed?"

"I have no idea," Jeremy said. "Of the eight birds we identified yesterday as being ill, two have died and the other six seem to be doing better. If the birds are getting milkweed somehow, we need to keep our eyes out for new cases of poisoning. The vet says the symptoms include drowsiness, lack of coordination, convulsions, and, eventually, death."

"That's why they appeared drunk," I realized.

"I noticed a few of the others acting tipsy. We'll have to keep an eye out for new cases as we go through our routine."

Jeremy and I worked side by side, feeding, inspecting, counting, and rotating the birds. By the end of the day, we'd found twelve more birds exhibiting the symptoms described. We isolated them, called the vet, and realized we were still dealing with a situation in which we came up with a different number every time we counted the birds. Today there were five fewer than yesterday, bringing the total to two less then we'd started with.

"Do you notice something strange about these birds?" I asked as we checked on the sick turkeys.

"Other than the fact that they're stumbling around and running into the sides of the pen?"

"I'm no turkey expert, but don't they look different to you? Smaller, for one thing."

"Yeah, I guess. Maybe they're younger than the others."

I remembered that the restaurant owner had sued Charles because he'd paid for heritage turkeys but was delivered regular ones. "What if someone is switching the turkeys?" I suggested. "That could account for the fluctuating numbers, as well as the milkweed if whoever is switching the birds doesn't know what they're doing."

"Switching?" Jeremy asked.

"Charles Tisdale raises a special breed of bird: heritage turkeys. His birds sell for five times what regular turkeys sell for. What if someone is slowly stealing the gourmet birds and replacing them with regular birds? There are a lot of turkeys on the property. It'd be hard to notice unless you were really a turkey expert, which we aren't."

"And the birds that are replacing the heritage ones are being poisoned before they even arrive," Jeremy caught on.

"Exactly."

"That could account for the strange numbers we're getting. Maybe our thieves can't count. They take birds and replace them with others but keep getting the numbers mixed up."

"My guess is that this might have been going on for a while. It's possible the switch could even have occurred at the time of butchering. At least while Charles, who would have noticed if there were strange birds on his property, was alive."

"It'd have to be the farm manager, or possibly one of the part-time workers," Jeremy deduced. "They could have switched them at the time of transport, or maybe the slaughterhouse is in on it."

"It's a brilliant scheme really," I acknowledged. "Charles has customers who pay upward of a hundred dollars a pop for his special birds. Someone steals the special birds and replaces them with common livestock at the last minute. Chances are, the average consumer might not even notice, but a restaurant owner like Raymond Wells noticed right away. What if Charles was justified in firing his staff? I figured he was ripping them off, but what if he started snooping around after the fiasco of the lawsuit and found out what they were doing?"

"Your theory makes sense," Jeremy acknowledged. "But how can we prove it?"

"We need to have someone who knows turkeys look at the sick birds," I said. I mentally reviewed the cast of characters in my mind. Oliver, Leroy, and Peggy would all have grown up on the farm, so I was willing to bet any of the three could tell the difference between a heritage and a regular bird. I knew that Brent spent a lot of time on the farm as well, although I didn't know how much exposure he had to the birds. I could probably ask any of the four, but I'd wanted to have a chat with Leroy, and perhaps this was the perfect opportunity.

"Any idea where Leroy is?" I asked.

"At the house with the others, I suppose."

"I'm going to see if I can find him. In the meantime, call the vet about the sick birds we've found, and see if our theory that they might have come into contact with milkweed prior to arriving at the farm holds up."

As I walked toward the house, I couldn't help but wonder how everything might be related: tipsy birds, fluctuating numbers, a dead farm owner, and his dead mistress. I guess there could be several explanations for the above set of variables, but for the life of me, I couldn't think of one.

I found Leroy in the living room, talking to Peggy and Margaret. The house had a somber feel, and the constant bickering that had been taking place between the heirs had been replaced by a fearful silence. It had most likely occurred to the group of leeches that they had a murderer in their midst. For those not guilty of the crimes, the possibility of another death must have been in the forefront of their minds.

"I was sorry to hear about Dolly," I offered as I walked into the room.

Margaret smiled at me, while Peggy and Leroy simply glared.

"Leroy," I began, "I was wondering if I could have a minute of your time. I have a question regarding the turkeys."

"Talk to Oliver," he snapped. "Our dearly departed father saw fit to make him estate executor. He might as well earn his pay."

"Oliver isn't available," I tried. "Please, it will just take a moment."

"Oh, very well." Leroy worked his girth into a standing position. "What can I help you with?"

"Something strange is going on with the birds," I revealed.

"Strange how?"

"We think someone might be switching your dad's gourmet birds for common turkeys, a few at a time."

"Why would someone be switching the birds?"

"I have no idea. I just know that something odd is going on and I'd like to get your opinion."

"Okay, lead the way."

"I overheard someone mention that you lived and worked on the farm until just a few years ago." I tried for a light tone as I led Leroy toward the pen where the sick birds had been quarantined.

"I devoted my life to this place. Lot of good it did me," Leroy grumbled.

"You decided on another career?" I fished.

"Let's just say that my old man and I didn't see eye to eye on a few things."

"That's too bad. It must be frustrating to devote your time and energy to something only to end up losing it in the end."

"Damn right it's frustrating."

I put on my most sympathetic face.

"I gave this farm the best years of my life and in the end the old man was going to sell it out from under me."

"He had plans to sell it before he died?" This was new information to me.

"He said he was too old for the daily grind. I tried to talk to him about selling it to me, but he said he had someone else in mind."

"Wow, that's awful. Do you know who?"

"He wouldn't say. Guess whoever talked my father into selling won't be getting it now. I hear there's a new buyer in the mix."

I realized he must be referring to Zak.

"So what do you think?" I asked Leroy as we arrived at the barn and I showed him the sick birds.

"Yup," he confirmed. "These are common fowl. You said they just showed up?"

"It seems that way." I filled him in on the erratic numbers, the milkweed poisoning, and Raymond Wells's lawsuit.

"My dad was an ass, but he was compulsive about his birds. If they were being traded out, it was after they left the farm. Dad personally checked the birds every day of his life. He would have noticed something like this right off."

"That's what we thought."

"I guess I should tell the sheriff about this. I'm supposed to meet him downtown in his office in thirty minutes anyway, to show him my airline stubs."

"Airline stubs?"

Leroy shrugged. "Guess he needs some type of proof as to when folks arrived on the property. I told him that I flew in Thursday afternoon, but apparently my word isn't good enough. Good thing I saved the damn tickets. Would have been a hassle to get the information otherwise."

I doubt it would have been a hassle at all to confirm Leroy's arrival with the careful record keeping airlines maintain. I suspect the good sheriff might have some other reason for requiring Leroy to produce the documents, but I didn't say as much. "I didn't realize you had an appointment. I'll let you get to it. Thanks for taking the time to look at the birds."

"Happy to help."

Based on what Leroy told me during our brief exchange, I realized that I could eliminate him as a suspect. He seemed confident that he could prove that he arrived Thursday afternoon, so he couldn't have killed Charles. I also now had confirmation that the sheriff's department was actively pursuing Charles's death as a murder. Otherwise why would they be looking for alibis from the family members on the property? It almost killed me to have Leroy fill the sheriff in on everything Zak, Jeremy, and I had discovered. I had a deeply felt need to be the one to put everything together and solve the mystery, but even I didn't want to stand in the way of finding justice for Charles and Dolly's deaths. I still hadn't figured out how the murder fit in with the hijacked turkeys. I supposed it was possible Charles found out what was going on and the person who was stealing the birds killed him to protect his secret, but why kill Dolly?

"I should get home and relieve Zak," I informed Jeremy. "Call me if you hear anything new. Chances are, our turkey thief, whoever he or she may be, will hear of our discovery and the replacing of turkeys will cease. Still, I'd be interested in getting the whole story."

"I'll keep my ears open," Jeremy promised.

Chapter 12

By the next day, Maggie was doing much better, able to nurse the puppies on her own. Zak had an appointment to sign the final paperwork on the estate but promised to look in on the dogs while I was gone. I was glad Zak was officially buying the house next to mine, but I missed his company on the long drive to and from the farm. At least I only had a few days left. The turkeys were being loaded for transport to the processing facility on Sunday, they would be slaughtered there on Monday, and they'd be distributed to customers who had prepurchased the birds on Tuesday. I couldn't believe it was going to be Thanksgiving on Thursday of next week.

"I tried to call you, but your cell was off," Jeremy said when he greeted me with a laugh. "It's nice to know some things never change. They've arrested Bill Parker and a couple of other guys for switching out the birds."

I remembered that Bill had been the farm manager.

"Did they confess to killing Charles and Dolly?"

"Quite the opposite. Bill and the others confessed to the switch, but everyone involved swears he isn't guilty of either death."

"Do we believe them?"

"I don't know, do we?" Jeremy asked. "You're the amateur sleuth. I'm just the sidekick."

I thought about the situation. "Okay," I said, working through the scenario, "Bill Parker has been Charles's farm manager for quite some time. He comes up with a plan to switch out the birds, making a tidy profit with each switch. He gets away with it for a while, probably only switching birds ordered by turkey novices who wouldn't notice. Everything is going well until he gets greedy when Raymond Wells places a large order during the slow season. Wells discovers the switch and sues Charles. Charles realizes what happened, settles out of court, then does his own investigation and discovers Bill's scheme."

"Makes sense."

"He fires Bill and his entire crew once he has his proof," I continued. "The question is, why would Bill come back a week later and kill Charles in his kitchen? He must have known that if the switch came out he'd be a suspect, so why continue with the ruse after we took over?"

"Maybe he, like everyone else, believed that Charles died by accident, and you and I, novices that we are, would never notice the difference between the birds."

"Exactly," I agreed. "If Bill killed him, he would know that Charles had been murdered and wouldn't have risked continuing to make the switches. He must have figured that, although he no longer controlled shipping and distribution, he could make a few bucks with the flock by switching them out before they were transferred. If he kept an accurate count and the turkeys he brought in weren't sick, it would have worked."

"Okay, so if Bill didn't kill Charles and Dolly, who did?" Jeremy asked.

"I don't know, but I intend to find out."

As Jeremy and I went through our tasks, which had become something of a routine, I tried to figure out what the connection might be between the deaths of Charles and Dolly. It occurred to me that there was a small chance—a very small chance—that the murders of these two individuals might not be related to either the turkey swap or Charles's will.

I supposed it was possible Dolly could have had another man in her life who killed both Dolly and Charles in a jealous rage. Dolly was more than forty years younger than Charles, so it made sense that she might have been getting a little something on the side. While this possibility seemed remote, it was worth exploring further. The problem with that complicated scenario was that I was running out of time. Once the heirs completed the meet and complain that was scheduled for the next afternoon, most, if not all of them, would probably leave.

I had to admit the complicated twists and turns in the investigation were giving my migraine a migraine. If we eliminated the idea of some sort of twisted love triangle, as I'd speculated, we were left with six of the original suspects: Mason Perot, Oliver and Olivia, Peggy and Margaret, and Brent. I had no idea if Mason had a motive, but he'd been acting somewhat secretive since I'd first met him, so I couldn't quite bring myself to remove him from the list. Oliver, Olivia, Peggy, and Margaret had really good reasons for wanting Charles dead. Brent's motive was less clearly defined, but I couldn't help but feel that the journal played into the picture.

As for opportunity, Oliver and Olivia lived close by, so they could easily have killed Charles and then returned home. Peggy and Margaret claimed they'd arrived after Leroy but could easily have arrived early, killed Charles, left, and then returned. I realized as I pondered the situation that I really didn't know how and when Brent had arrived, but I knew he had recently met with Charles, so perhaps he'd remained in the area. Zak had mentioned that he didn't have an alibi, so I'd assume Zak knew the answer to the question. If they all *could* have done it, how was I going to narrow things down?

Chapter 13

After completing my work at the farm, I climbed into my truck and headed home. It had been an exhausting day both physically and emotionally. I missed Charlie's presence in my everyday life and realized that I would be glad when this temporary job came to a close.

I knew Zak was keeping an eye on the dogs, so I decided to take a few minutes to pop in on my dad. I'd been meaning to thank him for his help on Sunday. I'd thought many times about our conversation, and for the first time in my life, I really understood that my dad had been hurt by my mother as much, if not more, than I had. I'm not sure why this had never really occurred to me before. I guess I was so busy playing the role of the poor, neglected little child that I'd never stopped to consider how my mother's total desertion of both of us would have affected him as well.

I slowed as I approached the store my grandfather, Pappy, had built from logs he'd milled himself. The building was dark, indicating that my dad must have closed early. It had been snowing on and off all day, and I imagined Dad had wanted to get home early to take care of any shoveling that might need to be attended to.

As I passed Donovan's, I pulled up alongside Trish's Treasures to say hi to Trish Carson, the middle-aged woman who owned and ran the touristy shop. Trish is considered to be a staple in our community, having lived here for forty-eight of her fifty-two years.

"I see you're getting a head start on your village," I commented to the short, pudgy woman, who was dressed in a dark green sweatsuit.

"The shop owners' committee finalized the story and I have the perfect pieces to depict my part. I just couldn't wait to get started."

Every year the shop owners along Main Street get together and devise a story that's played out through the tiny miniature villages displayed in each store's front window. If you view the displays from west to east, an original and charming story of small-town Christmas is conveyed. I knew the deadline for all the store owners to have their window displays complete was the day after Thanksgiving, but, like Trish, many get early starts on their masterpieces.

"Is that a new gazebo?" I asked. The scene coming to life in Trish's window depicted a park on the edge of the lake, much like our own little town center.

"Actually, I've had it for a while, but until this year the window scenes I've been assigned haven't really fit its inclusion."

"It's really beautiful. I can't wait to see the window when it's completed."

"We've missed you at the events committee meetings the past few weeks," Trish said, setting down the carousel and turning to face me.

"I've been a bit out of sorts since I lost my job. I'm working with Jeremy at a turkey farm in the valley this week, but I plan to attend the dinner next week, and the meeting the week after."

"Hometown Christmas is scheduled for December nineteenth through twenty-second. That's in just four weeks. The committee is counting on you to have everything ready and organized for the opening day," Trish reminded me.

"I know. Don't worry. I've been working on it. Gabe Turner is planning to run the sleigh rides again this year. I've spoken to him several times and can assure you he's dialed in and ready to go. Most of the food and craft vendors from last year have confirmed their intention to participate again this year. I have a few new recruits I'm still working with, but I should have all the contracts signed by the end of the month. I thought we'd set up the food court, kiddie games, and Santa's village in the community center. That way if we get a storm, folks can still enjoy the bulk of the festivities without having to wander around outside."

"If the vendors are all in the center, visitors will miss the windows," Trish pointed out.

"I thought of that. The community center is on the west end of town and the park is on the east. The bulk of the businesses who participate in the window displays are between the two. I plan to have various local artists provide holiday music in the gazebo. The staging for the sleigh rides will be in the park as well. I'm looking into putting up a big tent and having a second smaller food court, as well as some of the craft vendors, located on the east side of town. Unless the weather is really bad, I'm betting folks will walk between the two venues."

"And the children's play?"

"In the high-school gym."

Trish smiled. "I should have known you'd have things handled. The committee was getting nervous when you missed so many meetings, but I knew you wouldn't let us down. I'm glad to hear you plan to attend the community dinner as well. It's nice when the whole town gets together to share a meal. I'm bringing my Frito Bean Dish to the dinner again."

"I thought I'd do my Chicken Tortilla Casserole," I shared.

"I ran into Zak today." Trish continued to work on her window as we chatted. "He told me that rescue you adopted had her pups. Everything go okay?"

"We have four beautiful babies," I confirmed.

"My collie is getting on in years and I'm afraid I won't have her much longer. I've been thinking of getting a pup. I don't suppose any of yours are still available?"

"They're all available," I said. "Stop by any time and take a look."

"I will. By the way, did Hazel ever get a hold of you about the raccoon family that settled into her attic?"

I glanced at my phone, which was, predictably, turned off. "I guess my phone is off. I'll check my messages when I get home."

"She'd like to have them relocated before the snow we're expecting next week."

"I'll stop by in the morning and see what I can do," I promised.

Prior to my being fired, it was my job to monitor and control domestic animals in the area. The fact that Jeremy and I could always be counted on to handle wildlife issues as well had been an added bonus.

"You might call Ernie Young, too. I heard he found a stray dog in his shed. He mentioned that he was going to call you about finding a permanent placement for the little guy."

"I'll call him as well."

"It's nice to know the town has someone we can count on for all our pet needs," Trish complimented.

I thought about pointing out that it was no longer my job to place pets or remove raccoons from people's attics, but the truth of the matter was, I did what I did out of love for my four-legged friends and not because of a random although desperately needed paycheck. If there was a dog that needed a home or a family of raccoons that needed moving, I was happy to help out.

After finishing my conversation with Trish, I headed home. It was odd, but for some reason the prospect of a dog to place and raccoons to relocate left me feeling happier than I'd been since I'd been fired. I realized that I needed that sense of purpose in my life, and while babysitting turkeys and solving a mystery had turned out to be more interesting than I'd originally thought it would be, my destiny was here at the lake, high atop the mountain, dealing with the people and animals I was born to serve.

Chapter 14

Thursday was a day of surprises. I arrived at the farm early, thanks to Zak's willingness to accompany me and Ellie's offer to look in on the dogs. Today was the much-anticipated meeting of the heirs' lawyers, and as much as I wanted to be a fly on the wall, I knew there was really no excuse I could come up with to justify my presence in the house. Zak, on the other hand, had requested access to the property in order to inspect and survey his potential investment.

While Zak walked around, measuring walls and taking notes, Jeremy and I settled into what had become a predictable routine. Now that the turkey thieves had been arrested, our work went quickly, minus any incidence of missing or sick birds. We were close to completing our tasks for the day when an official-looking vehicle bearing a logo indicating that the occupant was from the department of fish and game pulled up.

"My name is Logan Cole," the driver of the vehicle introduced himself. "I'm here to take possession of these birds, effective immediately."

"Take possession?" I asked.

"They're evidence in a criminal investigation," he explained. "You'll be paid in full for the duration of your contract, but the birds are being relocated to one of our facilities."

"They won't be slaughtered?" I asked.

"While I'm not privy to their eventual fate, I can assure you that the birds won't be gracing anyone's table this particular Thanksgiving."

I smiled. A pardon, even a temporary one, seemed like a victory for the birds I had come to care about.

"I understand that you're under contract to care for the birds through the weekend. As I said, you'll be paid in full, although your employment is terminated immediately."

This just kept getting better and better. Of course, I had effectively run out of time to solve the murders of Charles Tisdale and Dolly Robinson. I was disappointed I wouldn't be able to complete my investigation but thrilled to be free of my daily commute and tedious tasks. Besides, with the holidays just around the corner, I had a million things to do if I was going to pull off the Christmas fund-raiser with the ease I'd tried to portray to Trish. I hadn't wanted to worry her, so I might have slightly overstated my level of readiness.

"The family is meeting with their attorneys," Logan informed us. "It you don't mind waiting until the meeting is over, I understand there's a check being cut for each of you."

"That's fine." I smiled. "We'll wait in the library."

Jeremy finished up in the yard while I went in search of Zak. My only hope of completing the task I had set for myself was to figure out who had done it before the meeting wrapped up. Not an easy task, since we really didn't have any new information, but maybe if we combined the brain power of the three of us . . .

"They're waiting for someone else to show," Zak informed us thirty minutes later as we observed the group through the same window in the library where Jeremy and I had watched them that first day.

"It looks like everyone is here except Oliver and Olivia," I commented as I considered each member of the eclectic group.

As before, Mason Perot was sitting at the head of the table. Holly sat next to him with a man who I assumed was her attorney to her right. Leroy was sitting to Mason's left, with Peggy beside him and Margaret to her left. It didn't appear that any of the three had invited legal counsel to attend. Brent was sitting at the opposite end of the table next to a woman in a dark green suit who I assumed was his attorney.

I studied each member of the group in turn. Mason looked bored with the whole affair. He seemed preoccupied and was communicating with someone on his cell phone. I couldn't tell exactly what he was doing, but he was so focused on the rectangular object that he barely looked up the entire time I watched him.

Leroy had a bottle of what looked like whiskey sitting in front of him. He spoke to Peggy a few times, but most of the wait he seemed content to down shot after shot. Of the people assembled, he was one of the few we'd cleared, yet based on his posture and binge drinking, he looked to be as nervous as anyone else.

Margaret spent most of the time chatting with Peggy. She appeared the most relaxed of those assembled, and I suspected that of the potential killers left on the list, she was the least likely to be guilty of the heinous crime.

Brent and his beautiful attorney got up from the table and retreated to a far corner of the room, where they seemed deep in discussion about something.

Holly sat quietly, staring at nothing in particular. She neither made eye contact with nor spoke to anyone else at the table and they, likewise, didn't speak to her. It occurred to me that she, like me, might suspect that one of the others had killed the mother she loved in spite of her faults.

"This is like watching a movie," Jeremy commented. "Any guesses as to who did it?"

I shook my head no. "I really don't know how we're going to narrow this down without new information," I said. "Oliver, Olivia, Peggy, Margaret, and Brent all lack alibis. Mason probably didn't do it, even though he *is* acting strangely."

"You started with fourteen suspects and narrowed it down to five." Jeremy tried to sound encouraging. "And we uncovered a conspiracy and saved hundreds of turkeys from holiday tables in the process. I'd say we had a good week."

"I really wanted to solve the murder," I insisted.

Zak turned to face me. "Let's go ahead and eliminate Mason. I don't think either of us believes he did it. If you considered the remaining five and had to choose the least likely suspect, who would it be?"

I turned to look at the group. "I suppose Margaret is the least likely. She seems open and genuine, and I've never picked up on any strange vibes from her."

"I agree," Zak said. "So then, who's the second least likely?"

I thought about Oliver and Olivia. Both gave me the creeps, but their stoic personalities didn't necessarily make them killers. Brent was friendly enough but appeared to have a secret, and there was that journal.

"I guess Peggy," I answered. "She has a good motive, but she doesn't strike me as the deranged-killer type."

"Okay, so let's focus on Oliver, Olivia, and Brent," Zak suggested. "What do we know about each of them?"

"Oliver recently found out that Charles might have killed his mother, Olivia was trying to blackmail Charles, which seems to have backfired, and Brent met with Charles the week before he died about an issue we are not privy to. We also know that he is in possession of Charles's journal."

"Okay," Zak prompted, "let's assume that all remaining suspects have motive to kill Charles, but who has a motive to kill Dolly?"

"Brent might want to murder Dolly in order to avenge his grandmother's heartbreak," I suggested. "Holly mentioned that her mother knew Olivia, but I have no idea if she ever met Oliver. Holly told me she thought Olivia asked for Dolly's help to get money out of Charles. Holly also revealed that Dolly didn't really have all that much influence over Charles, and even if she was able to get him to part with some of his riches, she would keep the money for herself rather than giving it to Olivia. I suppose if Dolly did somehow manage to get some money out of Charles but then kept it, that could give Olivia a motive to kill Dolly."

I watched as Oliver, Olivia, and a man dressed in a suit came into the conference room and motioned Mason over. They whispered for a few moments and then sat down at the table.

"I wish I could hear what they said."

"The man who came in told Mason that Oliver and Olivia have withdrawn their objections and agree to the will as written," Zak informed me.

"How do you know that's what he said?"

"I can read lips."

I looked at Zak with an expression that clearly communicated my disbelief.

"It's a thing." He shrugged.

During my exchange with Zak, Mason had addressed the crowd, who then stood up and filed out of the room. Talk about anticlimactic. I realized that the main reason I doubted Oliver and Olivia's guilt was because they *had* contested the will. I figured if they had been the killers, they would have wanted things wrapped up quickly. But now? Maybe one or both of them had done it.

I realized I had maybe an hour to work everything out before people started to leave. I needed inspiration and I needed it quick.

"Jeremy," I turned toward my former assistant, "you mentioned it was Oliver Tisdale who initially contacted you regarding the job."

"Yeah. He's the estate executor, so I suppose making sure the birds were cared for was part of his job."

"True, but don't you find it odd that Oliver hired *us* to care for the flock? I mean, sure, we have a background working with animals, but virtually no experience working with turkeys. The estate paid us a *lot* of money. Why wouldn't they try to find someone with more experience specific to turkeys?"

Jeremy stopped to consider this. "I never really thought about it. The guy calls me out of the blue and offers me a bunch of money to babysit a flock of dumb birds. I never stopped to question why."

"Someone who worked with turkeys on a regular basis would have recognized that the birds were being switched right away," I supplied. "What if Oliver was in on the theft? He knows he needs to hire someone credible for the rest of the group to go along with it, but he can't hire a turkey expert, who might upset his plans. He stumbles across us, who perfectly fit his needs."

"Oliver gets himself into financial trouble," Jeremy began. "He asks his dad for help and is refused, then gets the idea to hijack birds and replace them with others of a lesser quality. He grew up on the farm, so he would have been aware of the money to be made by such a switch. He approaches the farm manager, Bill Parker, who has his own ax to grind, and they begin harvesting turkeys for personal profit."

"Exactly." I could feel my excitement build as I narrowed in on the kill. "Everything goes as planned for a while, until Bill gets greedy and trades out the birds Raymond Wells was set to receive. Charles gets suspicious, does his own investigation, figures out what's going on, fires Bill, and threatens to cut Oliver out of the will. Oliver panics and kills his father before the new will can be signed."

"So where does Dolly fit in?" Jeremy asked.

"Maybe she saw something she shouldn't have?" I suggested, although even I doubted that was the answer.

"I don't know," Zak hedged. "If Oliver was in on the turkey switch, why wouldn't he just continue to switch them out after they left the property, like they had been? It would have been much easier to make the switch during transport or at the slaughterhouse than making it on the premises during the night."

"Yeah, I see what you mean," I grudgingly agreed. "If Oliver wasn't in on the switch, we're back to square one in terms of narrowing things down."

"So what do we do now?" Jeremy asked.

"I say we bluff," I said.

"Bluff how?" Jeremy asked.

"We pretend we have it figured out and see what happens. Jeremy, you go find the sheriff, and Zak, you find Mason and tell him we need to talk to him. I'll see if I can find out where the remaining suspects are."

"Are you sure about this?" Zak asked. "We could just let the sheriff take over from here."

"I don't figure we have a lot to lose," I pointed out. "We accuse one of the suspects in front of the others and see what happens. If the killer reveals his or her hand, the sheriff and his men are still here to handle things. If the killer doesn't come forward, we're no worse off than we are now."

"It's important to you to finish this?" Zak asked.

"Yeah, it is. I don't know why exactly, but it seems sort of wrong not to see this through."

"Okay, I'll get Mason."

"And I'll get the sheriff," Jeremy agreed.

As I wandered back through the house, I tried to figure out who was the most likely suspect. I needed to single out one member of the group to accuse. I thought back over everything we had discovered, which only confirmed that all three of the remaining suspects could just as well be the guilty party.

As I passed the stairway, I observed Oliver schleping armloads of bags down the stairs and into his car. I knew I shouldn't feel sorry for him. I'd pretty much decided he was the most likely suspect and probably the one I should accuse. Still, he'd had a tough life. Based on the information we'd uncovered, his mother had been sickly before her death. Afterward, six-year-old Oliver had been left alone with a father who, by all appearances, was a cold, heartless man. I could understand how Oliver could grow up bitter and resentful of the man who apparently had killed his mother. I watched him head up the stairs for another load of luggage. The look of resignation on his face was almost enough to make me decide to pick on one of the others.

"I told you the case with the shoes needed to go in next," Olivia said, appearing at the top of the stairs.

"I have it." Oliver raised a blue bag into the air.

"Not that bag, you idiot; the dark blue bag."

Oliver took a deep breath but went back up the stairs to make the exchange.

"Honestly, once I get my money I'm hiring someone with half a brain to take care of these things," Olivia added as Oliver followed her down the hall. "I can't remember the last time you didn't screw things up."

I paused at the bottom of the stairs as Oliver returned to a bedroom to fetch the proper bag. I hoped the sheriff would arrive before Oliver finished his chore.

"Are you looking for someone?" Holly asked when she and Brent walked into the room where I was standing.

"My friend Jeremy," I answered.

"I guess you'll be going now that the birds are being taken away."

"Yes, we've been given our final check. By the way, I was sorry to hear about your mom."

"Thank you. It's been a shock."

"Holly and I are heading into the parlor for a drink if you'd like to join us," Brent offered. I noticed the interest in his eyes. Some guys are always on the prowl in spite of the situation. The fact that Brent wasn't hurrying away most likely indicated that he wasn't the killer, but I would love for a way to slip his possession of the journal into casual conversation.

"Thanks, but I'll be leaving as soon as my friend arrives," I answered.

During our conversation Oliver had made several more trips down the stairs with baggage in various shades of blue. I was about to go to see what was keeping Jeremy and the sheriff when Oliver returned one final time with Olivia on his heels. It appeared that the couple was about to leave. I hadn't seen Jeremy or Zak since we'd parted, and the sheriff hadn't yet arrived. Should I stop them?

"I think I know who killed your father," I blurted out as Oliver opened the door of his car.

"You do?"

"Who may or may not have killed Charles is none of your concern." Olivia spoke up. "You were hired to do a job and were generously compensated. I suggest you leave before you bite off more than you can chew."

"I know your father planned to cut you out of his will," I told Oliver, fishing.

"My dad threatened to cut me out of his will every time I displeased him," Oliver said. "He wouldn't have done it. I know my father was irritated when I lost my investment, but I wasn't worried."

What?

I glanced at Olivia, who was making her way around to the driver's side of the car.

Suddenly that little nagging voice in my head began to scream to be heard. By all accounts Oliver was a weak and timid man who bowed down to the demands of his overbearing wife. Did it really make sense that he could have killed two people in cold blood? Olivia, on the other hand, was a real piece of work. She had been the one to try to blackmail Charles. Could she have been Bill's accomplice as well?

The idea that it was Olivia who had killed Charles began to take root in my mind. What if Olivia was actually the one behind the turkey swap? She wanted money from Charles and he wouldn't give it to her. Bill Parker couldn't even keep straight the number of birds he swapped. He didn't strike me as an evil mastermind.

If Olivia planned the swap and then killed Charles, why would she kill Dolly? I remembered Holly saying that her mother was only in a relationship with Charles for the money. What if tightwad Charles wasn't coming through to the degree Dolly expected? He was an old man. In my estimation, Dolly wouldn't waste a lot of time on a man from whom she wasn't getting a financial reward. What if Dolly and Olivia were in on the theft together?

Olivia slid into the driver's seat and started the car as Oliver and I spoke. She shoved it into gear and hit the gas before Oliver or I could respond. I pushed Oliver out of the way a second before I felt the impact of cold steel on my side.

Chapter 15

The light in the room was bright. Too bright. I didn't know where I was, but I was fairly certain it wasn't somewhere pleasant. I could hear people talking in the background, but I couldn't make out what they were saying. I struggled toward consciousness, but something was pulling me back.

"We'd like to keep her overnight for observation, but she should be fine in a day or two."

Day or two? Was someone hurt? I tried to move my leg and realized that the *someone* being referred to was probably me.

"Has she suffered any long-term damage?"

Dad?

"She's got a nasty cut on her leg, as well as quite a few minor abrasions, but nothing was broken, and there doesn't appear to be any internal bleeding. I'd say your daughter was very lucky."

Lucky? Are you kidding me? I felt like I'd been run over by a truck.

"We've given her a strong sedative. She'll most likely sleep through the night. Perhaps you should get some rest and come back in the morning."

"I'll stay with her."

Zak?

"Why don't you go back to the boathouse and stay with the dogs? You know if she was awake, she'd be worried about someone being with Maggie."

Damn right.

"Okay." The voice seemed a million miles away. "Call me if there's any change."

"I will. I promise."

I tried to figure out who was going to the boathouse and who was staying. I didn't suppose it mattered. The animals would be in good hands with either Zak or my dad. The doctor said I was going to be okay, but honestly, I was pretty sure I was dying. I wanted to open my eyes, but no matter how hard I tried, my body refused to obey. It made me sad that my days might come to an end before I could tell Zak that I've never *really* hated him and in fact have always loved him. On the other hand, I suspected he'd always known.

Chapter 16

The first thing I saw when I opened my eyes was Zak, sitting in the chair next to my bed.

"Good morning, sleepyhead. How do you feel?"

"Feel?"

I looked around the room and tried to figure out where I was.

"You're in the hospital," Zak answered my unspoken question. "Olivia Tisdale tried to run you down with her car."

"Based on the pain in pretty much every part of my body, I'd say she succeeded."

Zak smiled. "Almost. You managed to leap up onto the hood of her car, avoiding a much more serious injury."

"Oliver?" I was beginning to remember.

"You most likely saved his life."

"Is she . . ."

"In jail, thanks to you and some quick thinking. Looks like you figured out the mystery after all."

"I did?" I couldn't remember anything about that final day at that moment.

"You were the one who realized that Dolly and Olivia were in on the turkey swap."

"I was?" I struggled to focus my mind.

"Dolly was the mastermind behind the turkey swap," Zak reminded me. "Olivia contacted Dolly about using her influence to get Charles to fork over some of the money he was hording. Dolly knew Charles had money, but she had no idea how much until she talked to Olivia. That made her angry, since Charles had turned out to be a bit of a tightwad. Dolly didn't have as much influence over Charles as one might assume, but she realized there might be another way to get the money she felt she deserved."

"That's right." My brain was beginning to clear. "I suspected that Dolly approached the farm manager, Bill, about making the switch. Olivia found out and wanted in," I continued. "Dolly realized that Olivia could ruin a good thing for everyone involved, so she agreed to give her a cut of the profits. Everything was fine until Bill got greedy and Charles got suspicious. He did his own investigation and figured everything out. He fired his farm workers and threatened to disinherit Oliver for Olivia's part in the scheme. When Olivia thought Charles was really going to cut Oliver out of the will this time, she killed him. I have no idea why she killed Dolly."

"I spoke with the sheriff," Zak informed me. "You're actually pretty spot- on with your theory. It seemed that after Olivia killed Charles, Dolly got cold feet and was going to confess her part in the scheme, so Olivia killed her as well."

"Olivia confessed?"

"After a lengthy interrogation."

I smiled. It hurt to smile. Hell, it hurt to breath.

"I don't suppose you ever found out about the argument Brent had with Charles?"

"Sorry, no."

"I hate unanswered questions and loose ends."

"I guess there are just some things we'll never know," Zak offered.

"I guess. Can I go home?"

"Not until tomorrow, or possibly Sunday," Zak informed me. "The doctor thinks you have a concussion. After the trauma to your body, they want to keep an eye on you."

"The animals?"

"Your dad is staying at the boathouse. Maggie is fine, and Charlie is on his way here."

"Charlie is coming?" Suddenly I felt a whole lot better.

"Sure, why not? Charlie is a therapy dog, after all, and I convinced the good doctor that you were in need of therapy."

Charlie burst into the room and jumped up onto my bed. As a therapy dog, he'd been trained to wait until he was ordered to jump up onto a bed. I guess I should have corrected his behavior, but I was so happy to see my little bundle of fur that the searing pain where he stepped on my sore arm was barely noticeable.

"Can he stay?" I asked hopefully.

"He can only be in the room when I'm here to oversee the visit, but I'm not going anywhere," Zak promised.

"How can I ever thank you?"

"Get better. I have a surprise for you that I've been dying to give you."

"A surprise? What kind of surprise?"

"You'll see."

"Zak, I'm an injured woman at death's door. You shouldn't tease me."

"I'm not teasing you. Now, where do you stand on gin rummy?"

"I kill at rummy."

I relaxed into the pillows piled behind me as Zak dealt the cards he'd brought. They say that in the moments before you die your life flashes before you. I don't know if that's true, but I do know that in the few seconds between being hit by Olivia's car and blacking out, it was Zak's smile that flashed through my mind. I'm not sure what, if anything, that might mean for our future, but for the first time in my life I'm open to setting aside my ridiculous grudge and finding out.

Chapter 17

By the time Thanksgiving rolled around, I was truly thankful for everything and everyone in my life. It had started to snow as Charlie and I made our way down the beach to Zak's house that morning. The forecast called for up to three feet over the next few days. I only hoped my leg would have healed enough to hit the slopes by the time the resorts opened in a week or so. Luckily, none of my injuries were serious and, except for some ugly bruising, I was almost back to new.

"What smells so wonderful?" I asked as Charlie and I walked in from the beach.

"Sticky buns. They're my mom's recipe. She made them every Thanksgiving when I was growing up."

"They smell fantastic."

"They are fantastic. Coffee?"

"Please."

"It seems like you're getting around better today."

"I still have a few aches and pains, but overall I'm feeling much better." I accepted the coffee Zak gave me, then slid onto one of the tall stools lining the kitchen counter. I took a sip of the rich brew as Zak stuffed the bird. Soft jazz played in the background, giving the room a cozy feel. "I'm really looking forward to getting together with the whole family this afternoon, but I have to admit having the morning to ourselves is nice."

"I'm glad you suggested it," Zak agreed. "It's nice to spend time with just the two of us."

"Better make that four," I teased, nodding Charlie and Lambda, who were keeping warm in front of the brick fireplace that separated the kitchen from the informal dining area.

"Okay, four." Zak grinned. "I wasn't going to mention this unless I had news to share, but I drove down the mountain yesterday and took Jeremy and his new buddy Pike to lunch."

"Jeremy and Pike are buddies?"

"I guess they struck up a friendship while Jeremy was working at the farm. He didn't like hanging out with the heirs in the evenings, so he'd head over to Pike's for whiskey and poker after he finished for the day."

"I'm surprised he didn't mention it."

"He said you would have given him a bad time about the poker."

Jeremy was right. I probably would have given him a bad time for gambling when he had bills to pay and a baby on the way. Did I mention I tend to be a buttinsky?

"So why did you take them to lunch?"

"I thought maybe Pike could shed some light on the final piece of the Charles Tisdale murder."

"Brent's argument with Charles," I guessed.

"Pike confirmed that Charles didn't tell him the details of the argument he had with Brent, but when I explained about the journal, he remembered something Charles had said."

"Go on."

"Pike mentioned that Charles was upset with Brent because he found something he shouldn't have. After I told him about the journal and what it said about his abuse as a young man and his contribution to Amelia's death, Pike shared that Charles was very secretive about his life prior to meeting Amelia. He was ashamed of the abuse he suffered at his father's hand and didn't want anyone to know. Pike revealed that the only reason he knew anything at all about his life as a child and young man is because Charles said some things during a late night of heavy drinking."

"Why would he be ashamed of being abused?" I asked. "It actually explains a lot about his personality."

"Charles lived his life from a position of strength and authority. He believed in hard work and making your own way. He was ashamed of the fact that he'd once let himself be a victim."

"So when Brent found the journal, Charles must have been afraid he'd spill the beans about his deepest, darkest secret," I theorized.

Zak shrugged. "It's a guess. I suppose we'll never know for certain, but the explanation makes as much sense as any."

It warmed my heart that Zak had gone to so much trouble to try to unravel the final piece of the puzzle. The murder had been solved and the guilty party brought to justice, but I had to admit that having this huge gaping question mark left me feeling less than satisfied.

"The oven is binging," I informed him.

"Sticky buns are done. Refill on your coffee?"

"I'd love one."

Spending the morning alone with Zak as we prepared the holiday feast felt oddly domestic in a couple sort of way. I'm still not sure how I feel about my growing attraction to the man I realize I probably already love, but my heart tells me that he's a good and caring man who will lovingly deal with my at times irrational emotions and often times impulsive and erratic behavior. I'm not sure why I've always assumed Zak's kindness toward me was some sort of twisted ploy to irritate me. During the past few weeks I've come to realize that Zak's kindness is simply kindness.

"The turkey is stuffed and in the oven, the potatoes are peeled and ready to boil, the pies are cooling in the pantry. What else do we need to do?" I asked Zak several hours later.

"I think we're good for now. The others won't be here for a couple of hours, so I think this is a good time to give you the surprise I promised you."

"Surprise?" I tried to act like I'd forgotten all about Zak's comment in the hospital, but the truth of the matter was that I'd thought of little else since being released.

"We'll need to go for a drive," Zak informed me.

"But the food . . ."

"Will be fine. I just need to make one quick phone call. Grab your coat. We won't be gone long."

Zak made his call and then helped me into his truck. My leg was better but still far from completely healed, and climbing into the cab presented a bit of a problem. He turned the heater on high and the radio to a station playing soft jazz. It was snowing lightly, and the warmth and coziness of the truck as Zak slowly made his way into town made me feel happy and content. Zak hummed along to the music until we reached the outskirts of the downtown section of our little village. He pulled the truck over to the side of the road and handed me a scarf.

"What's this for?" I wondered.

"It's a blindfold."

I was skeptical, but I let Zak tie the scarf around my eyes before he put the truck into gear and continued on.

"Don't you think this is a bit over the top?" I asked.

"Probably."

"Is it far?"

"No, we're just about there."

I tried to figure out where we were going. I suppose I should have paid more attention to the directions of Zak's turns. I'd lived in Ashton Falls my whole life, so I was confident that if I had paid attention, I would have figured out the general location of our secret destination.

After several minutes Zak slowed down, then came to a stop. He got out of the truck and walked around to open the door on my side. He took my arm and gently helped me to the ground. He led me several steps forward and then stopped. "Close your eyes," he instructed.

Zak slipped the blindfold off my closed eyes. "Okay, open them."

I held my breath as I slowly opened my eyes. I stood in front of the old shelter where I'd poured out my heart and soul to save numerous animals over the years. It was dark, but the facility looked much as I remembered it: old and weathered, with a T-shaped building and a large outdoor area with pens and cages.

"Do you like it?"

"Like it?"

"Look at the sign," Zak instructed.

The old sign had read Ashton Falls Animal Control and Rehabilitation Shelter, while the new sign simply said ZOE'S ZOO. I looked at Zak. "What did you do?"

Zak shrugged. "The county wanted to sell the building, the town needs a shelter, and I was looking for an investment."

"You own the building?" I was still trying to wrap my head around the whole thing.

"A third of it," Zak admitted. "We have a silent partner who insisted on investing."

"Who?"

"Our silent partner would like to remain both silent and anonymous," Zak said.

"Who owns the final third?" I had to ask.

"You do."

"I do?" I couldn't have been more shocked if he'd told me the final third was owned by Santa Claus. "Our silent partner and I put up the money for the business, and we figured you could run it."

"You want me to run it?" I knew I wasn't making any sense, but I was in shock.

"With a little help," Zak said, as Jeremy walked toward us from behind the building.

"Isn't it great?" Jeremy gushed. "We can pick up where we left off without the county breathing down our necks."

I looked at Jeremy and tried to comprehend what he was saying. His shaggy brown hair hung in his eyes, but his grin of pure joy was unmistakable. Then I looked at Zak and began sobbing like a baby. In a million years I couldn't have prepared myself for the flood of emotions that consumed me when the full impact of Zak's very generous gift finally sank in. I must have started to crumble since the next thing I knew, Zak had picked me up and I was being held in his arms as I cried the tears that I'd restrained for so long.

"Zoe, are you okay?" I heard Jeremy's concerned voice.

I nodded my head but continued to sob as I wrapped my arms around Zak's neck and held on for dear life.

"These are tears of joy?" Zak sounded uncertain.

I hated to see the concern in his eyes, but I still couldn't speak.

"We can open as soon as we get the permits," Jeremy said. "Levi and Ellie pitched in and got the place cleaned up."

I sobbed harder.

Zak shifted me slightly in his arms. I figure my weight wasn't the issue as much as the fact that his shirt was soaked through to his skin with the tears I'd shed. He handed me a tissue, which I gratefully accepted. Once I pulled myself together, I allowed Zak to set me gently on the ground.

"Better?" Zak smiled.

"Than I've ever been in my life."

And I was.

Recipes from
The Trouble with Turkeys

Zak's Mac and Cheese
Ellie's Fettuccini Alfredo
Zoe's Chicken Tortilla Casserole
Hazel's Frito Bean Dish

Rosie's Pilgrim Pie
Zak's Easy Sticky Buns
Ellie's Carrot Cake
Zoe's Pumpkin Snickerdoodles

Zak's Easy Mac and Cheese

1 box – 16 oz Penne Pasta
4 Chicken Breasts cooked and cubed
1 can of Campbell's Cream of Cheddar soup
1 can of Campbell's Nacho Cheese Soup
(you can use two cans of either if you like your casserole more or less spicy)
1 jar (16oz) Alfredo sauce (any brand)
2 cups shredded Cheddar Cheese
1 cup grated Parmesan Cheese
¾ cup milk
1 cup cashews (or more if you'd like)
Salt and pepper to taste
Cheddar cheese crackers

Boil pasta according to directions on box (10 – 12 min)

Meanwhile mix cooked and cubed chicken, soups, cheeses, Alfredo sauce, milk, cashews, and salt and pepper together in a large bowl.

Drain pasta when tender and add to chicken mixture. Stir until well mixed.

Pour into a greased 9 X 13 baking pan. Top with crumbled cheddar cheese crackers.

Bake at 350 degrees for 30 minutes.

Ellie's Fettuccini Alfredo

Melt 1 cube butter (real butter no substitutions) in sauce pan over medium heat

When melted add:
½ 8oz package cream cheese
2 cups of heavy whipping cream
Stir until cream cheese is completely dissolved

Slowly add:
1½ cups grated Parmesan Cheese (the good stuff)
1 cup grated Romano Cheese (add slowly don't let it clump)
Stir until smooth

Add:
1 tsp of ground nutmeg
½ tsp of garlic powder
Add salt and pepper to taste (Ellie uses white pepper)

Note: if you like your sauce thicker you can add additional Parmesan and if you like it thinner you can add additional cream.

Pour over fettuccini, tortellini, or any other pasta (fresh from the refrigerator section is best)

Zoe's Chicken Tortilla Casserole

4 Chicken breasts cooked and cubed
2 Cans (7 oz) diced green chili's (Zoe uses Ortega)
1 Can (10 oz) chicken broth
1 Can (10 oz) cream of mushroom soup
1 Can (10 oz) Cream of Chicken Soup
1 large can or 2 small cans sliced black olives
1 can (15 oz) corn drained

Combine everything above and set aside

1 pkg corn tortillas
2 cups shredded Cheddar Cheese

Layer half or tortillas, half of soup, and half of cheese in greased 9X13 baking pan

Repeat with second half

Bake at 350 degrees for 30 minutes

Hazel's Frito Bean Dish

1 can (15 oz) chili with beans (any brand)
½ chopped onion
1 can (7 oz) chopped green chili (Hazel uses Ortega)
1 can (4 oz) sliced black olives
1 can (10 oz) Campbell's Nacho Cheese Soup

Mix everything above together.

I bag Fritos (plain or Chili Cheese)

Layer chili mixture with Fritos in greased baking pan

Bake at 350 for 30 min

Rosie's Pilgrim Pie

1 Premade Pie Shell

2 eggs
1 cup brown sugar
1 cup dark corn syrup
1 tsp vanilla
2 Tbs butter, melted
1/8 tsp salt
1/2 cup grated coconut
1/2 cup rolled oats
1/2 cup pecans

Beat eggs. Blend in sugar, corn syrup, vanilla, butter, and salt. Stir in coconut, oats and pecans.

Pour into pie shell.

Bake at 400 degrees for 15 minutes. Reduce oven to 350
degrees and bake for 30 minutes.

Check with knife to see if pie is set. If not set bake until set.

Zoe's Pumpkin Snickerdoodles

1 cup butter at room temperature
1 cup granulated sugar
½ cup light brown sugar
¾ cup canned pumpkin
1 large egg
2 tsp vanilla extract
3¾ cups flour
1½ tsp baking powder
½ tsp salt
½ tsp ground cinnamon
¼ tsp ground nutmeg

For the coating:
½ cups sugar
1 tsp cinnamon
½ tsp ground ginger
Dash of allspice

Whip together butter and sugars until creamy. Add pumpkin, egg, and vanilla. Mix well. Add dry ingredients and mix well.
Refrigerate for at least 1 hour

In a separate bowl mix the sugar and spices for the coating. Roll chilled dough into one inch balls. Roll in coating.

Bake on ungreased cookie sheet at 400 degrees until lightly brown (around 12 minutes)

Zak's Easy Sticky Buns

Made with frozen bread dough and simple ingredients you probably have on hand. While there are several steps they go quickly and are simple to make. Quick and yummy!

Take 6 tablespoons butter and melt in a pan. When melted add 3/4 cup brown sugar and 1/4 cup corn syrup. Stir mixture over medium low heat bringing to a boil.

When at a full boil remove from heat. Do not over boil. The syrup will set up to hard.

Pour into the bottom of a 13x9 inch pan. Add 3/4 cup of chopped pecans on top of the syrup mixture. Set aside.

In a pie pan melt 4 tablespoons of butter. In a separate pie pan mix 1/2 cup sugar and 1 1/2 tablespoons of cinnamon. Set aside.

Take 1 1/2 loaves of thawed frozen bread dough and cut into 12 equal pieces. Take each piece and roll into a tube. Take each piece of dough and roll first into the melted butter and then in the cinnamon sugar. Tie the piece into a knot and set in the prepared baking pan on top of the syrup pecan mixture.

Put the rolls in a warm place to rise until it fills the pan.

Bake at 400 degrees for 20 to 25 minutes. The rolls are done when they are nice and brown. Make sure the rolls are cooked through. Do not undercook.

When the rolls are baked, take out the pan.
Cover the top of the pan with a foil lined cookie sheet. Invert the pan onto the cookie sheet. The pecan mixture will seep down on top of the rolls.

Serve warm. Makes 1 dozen.

Ellie's Carrot Cake

2 Cups Sugar
3 Eggs
3 Cups Finely Shredded Carrots
1 8 oz Package softened cream cheese
1 ¼ Cup Vegetable Oil
2 Cups Flour
2 Tbs Ground Cinnamon
2 tsp Baking Soda
1 tsp Salt
1 Can 8 oz Crushed Pineapple well drained
2 Cups Walnuts Chopped

Beat eggs and sugar together until blended. Add carrots, cream cheese, and oil. Beat until smooth. Add dry ingredients. Stir in pineapple and nuts. Pour into greased 9X13 baking dish. Bake at 350 for 55-60 minutes.

Frosting:
¾ Cup butter softened
6oz cream cheese softened
1 Tbs vanilla
3 Cups Powdered sugar

Whip together – frost cake when cool and top with pecans

Books by Kathi Daley

Come for the murder, stay for the romance.

Buy them on Amazon today.

Paradise Lake Series:

Pumpkins in Paradise

Snowmen in Paradise

Bikinis in Paradise

Christmas in Paradise

Puppies in Paradise – *February 2015*

Zoe Donovan Mysteries:

Halloween Hijinks

The Trouble With Turkeys

Christmas Crazy

Cupid's Curse

Big Bunny Bump-off

Beach Blanket Barbie

Maui Madness

Derby Divas

Haunted Hamlet

Turkeys, Tuxes, and Tabbies

Christmas Cozy – *November 2014*

Alaskan Alliance – *December 2014*

Road to Christmas Romance:

Road to Christmas Past

Kathi Daley lives with her husband, kids, grandkids, and Bernese Mountain dogs in beautiful Lake Tahoe. When she isn't writing, she likes to read (preferably at the beach or by the fire), cook (preferably something with chocolate or cheese,) and garden (planting and planning not weeding). She also enjoys spending time on the water when she's not hiking, biking, or snowshoeing, the miles of desolate trails surrounding her home.

Kathi uses the mountain setting in which she lives, along with the animals (wild and domestic) that share her home, as inspiration for her cozy mysteries.

Visit Kathi:
Facebook at Kathi Daley Homepage
Twitter at Kathi Daley@kathidaley
Webpage www.kathidaley.com

Made in the USA
Middletown, DE
14 August 2018